Hell on Heels:

My Sister's Keeper

Hell on Heels:

My Sister's Keeper

Brittani Williams

www.urbanbooks.net

Urban Books, LLC
97 N18th Street
Wyandanch, NY 11798

ISBN 13: 978-1-60162-596-0
ISBN 10: 1-60162-596-0

First Trade Paperback Printing May 2014
Printed in the United States of America

10 9 8 7 6 5 4 3 2 1

Distributed by Kensington Publishing Corp.
Submit Wholesale Orders to:
Kensington Publishing Corp.
C/O Penguin Group (USA) Inc.
Attention: Order Processing
405 Murray Hill Parkway
East Rutherford, NJ 07073-2316
Phone: 1-800-526-0275
Fax: 1-800-227-9604

Hell on Heels:

My Sister's Keeper

A novel by

Brittani Williams

Part One

The Past

Chapter One

Sapphire

I Wanna Rock

1991

Just like the lyrics, I was popping my pussy and not planning on stopping until my G-string was full of all the cash he carried. The private room in the Velvet Rope was the place to be. Here you could put all of your skills to use without any distractions. As the sounds of Uncle Luke's "I Wanna Rock" blared through the speakers, my ass cheeks were taking turns jiggling in front of my best customer.

Enzo was his name. Standing well over six feet tall, all muscle with a smooth Hershey's chocolate skin tone, most women would jump his bones without a second thought. Granted, he was fine as all hell but looks weren't enough for me. I mean yeah, he had cash for days, but the things that I'd heard about him through the grapevine were enough to make me afraid. Not only was I afraid that he'd break my heart, but my face if I didn't abide by his rules. He's been known to bust a bitch in the mouth even in public, and I wasn't trying to go out like that. Despite it all, there was just something magnetic about him, and I couldn't stop myself from being mesmerized every time he stepped in the building. Still, I decided to play hard to get as long as he kept chasing. I mean why not? At least he'd appreciate it when he got it.

"What's so special about this pussy that I need to pay for it?" Enzo asked while keeping his eyes steady on my gyrating torso just two feet in front of him.

"You've already dropped five hundred dollars tonight and all you've done was look at it. Hell you haven't even smelled the pussy yet. If you have money to spend on watching me why not invest a little more to fuck me?" I yelled over the loud music.

Enzo sat there staring at my Coke-bottle frame and protruding camel toe. I could see the bulge in his pants quickly growing as he squirmed a little in his seat. He'd been spending at least two stacks every weekend just to watch me dance in a private room; this weekend was no different.

"If you come home with me after your shift I'll give you much more. I want the pussy trust me; I just don't want to treat you like a prostitute," Enzo replied.

"I told you that's against the rules. If I come home with you, I'd have to quit my job. Are you ready to take care of me?" I asked while continuing the lap dance that he'd paid me for.

"I got'chu. I told you before: I have enough bread to support a small village. Shit, if you get down with me you'll never have to shake your ass for money again. I'm being real. I come pay for these private shows so other niggas won't get to touch what I already consider to belong to me. I just want you to stop playing games wit' a nigga and give me what I need."

"What'chu need?" I asked with raised eyebrows.

"You heard me," he replied, grabbing a hold of his crotch while discussing the matter at hand.

"I'll have to think about it, Enzo," I said softly. I was afraid of him and the trouble that followed wherever he went. There had been at least two shootouts in the very same club when he and his rivals went to war.

"Think quick because I'm not gonna' keep beggin'. Trust me there's no shortage of pussy around for a nigga like me," he said as he sat up in his seat.

"Enzo, I'm sure you can get any woman you want so I know moving on to the next bitch would be easy. Clearly, it's something that I have that they don't," I spoke with confidence.

"Oh, yeah? Well, I guess I wouldn't know, would I, since I haven't, in your words, even 'smelled the pussy.' But I got'chu. You wanna play this game and I'm not playing it no more. I got people to see and bitches to do, so I'll see you around, all right?" he said as he stood from his seat, reached in his pocket, and retrieved another one hundred dollar bill. He looked at me and threw it in my direction before turning his back and walking out of the VIP room.

I stood there for a second before bending down to pick up the bill from the floor. I shook my head before walking out of the room and going to the dressing room. A few other women sat at different stations applying makeup, fixing their hair, and gossiping. I walked over to the free station at the far end of the room with a puppy-dog face. I was upset that I hadn't just followed my heart and gone with him. At this point, I felt that I'd screwed up any chance that I had with Enzo. Eliza, another dancer, walked over to me and bent over to look into the mirror.

"What's wrong, girl? Your night is ending early I see. Where is your high roller?" Eliza asked while fixing the flyaways on her hair.

"He left," I replied.

"This early? What happened?" she asked with raised eyebrows.

"He kept pestering me about going home with him and I'm not sure I'm comfortable with that."

"Comfortable? Girl, you work in a strip club shaking your ass and flashing your pussy for money. This nigga has spent thousands of dollars on you and you're afraid to give him some? Girl, if I were you I'd be at his crib bouncing on that dick right now and leaving with a fat-ass clutch full of money." She laughed while adjusting her bra.

"I'm afraid that I'm going to like him. I'm not trying to fall in love," I said honestly.

"Girl, I know you're young but if you're gonna catch feelings for every nigga who throws you some change this might not be the profession for you. There is too much money to be made for that love shit. Girl, get yourself together and get out on the floor and do what you do best. I'll see you out there," she said before walking out of the dressing room.

I looked over at the other girls who were giggling and whispering, probably about me. I had learned early on that it was better to bite my tongue versus fighting every chick who had something negative to say. True, I did get naked and dance for men every night but I never thought of myself the way that the other women did. I wasn't about to prostitute myself or be made to feel like one. At that point I wasn't in the mood to go out on the floor so I put on my clothes, grabbed my bags, and headed out of the dressing room.

As I walked through the club I noticed Enzo getting a lap dance from none other than Eliza. He looked over at me, smiled, and then placed a few bills into her G-string. Instead of embarrassing myself or causing a ruckus in the club I shook my head and walked out quietly. As I waved good-bye to the bouncer I paused. I couldn't just walk away quietly. *What the hell am I doing?* I thought. Quiet wasn't one of my characteristics, especially when I felt like I was being disrespected.

"Could you hold this bag behind the desk for me? I forgot something," I said as I handed the door attendant my bag. "Thanks. I'll be right back."

Walking back into the club I spotted Enzo being escorted to the private room in the back. I briskly walked across the floor until I was standing right outside of the room. I nodded at the bouncer who stood in front of the door before speaking. "Hey, I think I dropped my earring inside. I just need to run in real quick."

"All right, just stay out the way; it's a couple dancers working."

"I will," I replied before going in. I took a deep breath preparing myself for the altercation because I knew what I'd come to do. I wasn't about to allow that backstabbing bitch to steal him from right under me. I walked over to where Eliza was straddling Enzo, grinding her crotch into his jeans. Without warning, I grabbed a handful of Eliza's hair and pulled her down to the floor. Immediately I began punching and kicking her in the face and torso. Eliza screamed as she tried to gather up the strength to stand up but I knocked her back down each time. Enzo, at first sitting still, was now trying to separate Eliza from my death grip. After the bouncer entered and intervened they were able to pull her loose.

"You dirty bitch! You couldn't even wait until I left, could you?" I yelled.

"You didn't want him so why let a good specimen go to waste?" she replied with a laugh.

I struggled to get away from the bouncer. "So is this what you wanted? To make me jealous, Enzo?" I yelled.

Enzo nodded without a vocal response, only frustrating me more.

"You know what? Fuck you and fuck this." I snatched away from the bouncer and stormed out of the club. I walked toward my car and fumbled with my keys until

ഗ   ⅉ the ground. I was angrier with myself than
          ᷐h either of them. I'd let my own fears and
          ᷐ties stop me from pursuing him. I bent down to
          ᷐p the keys and was startled when Enzo appeared
ᵇ᷐ ᷐ᵈ me.

"So you had to see me with another chick before you decided that you wanted me?"

"Enzo, I don't have anything to say to you, okay?"

"I don't need you to speak," he said as he pushed me up against the car and forcefully kissed me.

For the first time I was able to feel his lips and the excitement sent a signal through my body that made me shiver. His dick was rock hard and practically bursting through his jeans. The closer he got the more it poked me. I didn't try to fight him. At that moment I wanted him just as much as he wanted me.

"Take me home with you," I spoke once we separated.

"I thought you'd never ask that." He smiled. "Your car or mine?" He laughed.

"Yours of course."

He laughed before signaling with his hand in the direction of his car. We walked over and I smiled at the all-black Range Rover parked near the rear of the parking lot. I'd heard that Enzo had bank but this ride was confirmaion of that. Only rich white men and drug dealers could afford vehicles that expensive. I stepped inside after he walked around to the passenger side and opened the door for me. Once inside, we remained quiet, both of us obviously unsure of what to say to the other. I was thinking about the night's events and wondering if I'd made the right decisions by coming with him.

"You know, your stage name should be Mayweather the way you were in there throwing jabs." He laughed. "I've had a lot of women fight over me in the past but never a woman I haven't even been intimate with. You shocked the hell out of me."

"Well, it really wasn't even about you; it was the principle. She knew what she was doing and she did it purposely to get at me. I don't like shady bitches like that."

"Oh, so it wasn't about me, huh? If it wasn't about me then why are you here with me now?"

"Because I like you. I was just afraid of you," I spoke with a smile.

"Afraid of what?" he asked.

"Your life, the rumors, all of it. I was just scared, okay?" I replied honestly.

"Well, no point in dwelling on all of that. You're here now and I'm glad." He reached across the seat and placed his hand on my thigh.

I looked down at his hand and smiled. I'd convinced myself that I'd made the right move and I planned to give exactly what he'd been asking for. He could fuck me all over his place or anywhere else for that matter. I wasn't playing anymore and I wanted him to know it. Fuck waiting. I set my bag down on the floor out of the way and slid his hand off of my thigh. He looked over at me but didn't speak. I reached over and grabbed the belt of his pants and unbuckled it.

"What are you doing?" he asked with a devilish grin.

"Giving you what'chu need. You asked; now I'm going to deliver." I unzipped his jeans and his hard dick made its way through his boxers. I was excited because he was working with the tools I was sure to enjoy. I took the tip of my index finger and rubbed the tip of his dick, removing the small puddle of pre-cum, and quickly licked it off of my finger. With his left hand on the wheel he swerved a little but quickly regained control of the car. I smiled briefly before wrapping my thick-ass lips around it and sliding my tongue down the shaft, tapping the back of my throat with the head.

"Goddamn, girl, you're gonna make me crash," he moaned.

I could feel him picking up speed as I sucked and slurped on his ten-inch stick. It throbbed inside of my mouth as I continued to do one of the things I did best. Giving great head was an art and I'd mastered it, or so I'd been told. Soon I could feel the car slow to a complete stop and he quickly moved me away. I wasn't sure why he'd stopped me until I sat up completely and realized we were parked in a driveway.

"Come on, get out," he said as he got out of the car not bothering to conceal his dick, which was stiff as a board.

I got out of the car and walked around the front only to be met by him in the center. Without speaking he lifted my dress, pushed me over toward the hood of the car, and rammed his dick inside of me from behind. It was pitch black outside. Only the motion light from his driveway shined on us like a spotlight. I didn't care if we could be seen. His dick felt so good that I felt myself cumming within seconds of contact.

"Is this what you wanted?" I asked breathlessly.

He didn't respond. He was palming my breasts with both hands and fucking me with force. You could hear his body slapping up against mine over the night sounds of the crickets. The heat from the car hood had me sweating bullets but I couldn't stop him. I didn't want to. He continued to pound me from behind for what felt like an hour until he quickly removed his dick and pushed me to the ground just in time to cum in my mouth. Now, I know most people would call me every ho in the book for this, but, hell, I worked in a strip club so I was far from conservative. He let out a loud sigh and smiled as I rose from my squatted position.

"I'm not done. I'm about to wax that ass all over this house." He slapped me on the ass and guided me toward the door.

I smiled as I was satisfied with my decision and I was looking forward to the long night ahead of me.

Chapter Two

Shekia

In Her Shadow

I wasn't excited; as a matter of fact I didn't give a shit! I mean really, every time she decided to visit everyone acted as if the Queen of England were arriving. Yeah, you might be thinking I was just the jealous baby sister, but that couldn't be further from the truth. Honestly, there wasn't anything about Milan that I envied. In my eyes, she was a fuckup who almost got her act together. I didn't give a damn whether she'd become a millionaire; your past is your past. You could try to run from it, but you'll never really escape it. So who am I? I'm sure that's your next question. I'm Shekia, who most would have called a plain bitch. I was cool with that title, because I wore it well and one thing you could never say was that I took anyone's crap.

Thinking back to my childhood, I couldn't remember a time when I genuinely liked my sister. She always had a huge head and swore her shit didn't stink. When my mother shipped her ass to Atlanta I was ecstatic. I was finally rid of her and her funky-ass attitude. Five years later, she was on her way back to Philly for good and I'd already prepared myself for a fight. I was great at the fifty-two fake out, so from the outside you'd believe we were the best of friends. If only people knew the real story. I was twelve years old when she left and so much had changed since then. I was a different person and I was certain she wouldn't like who I'd become.

Anyhow, it was the day before her return and I went about my day as planned. Typically, school wasn't on the agenda, but I hadn't been able to get in touch with my boyfriend, Mannie, and I wasn't about to sit outside the door like a lost puppy. I walked into the building feeling out of place. I couldn't remember the last time that I was actually present in homeroom. Immediately I was bombarded with side eyes and twisted lips. I didn't have too many female friends and most of the girls in school hated me.

"Well, if it isn't Miss Brooks. Haven't seen you in a while, thought you had transferred," Mr. Wilson said with a half smile.

"Ha-ha, very funny," I replied, annoyed. Honestly, why the hell did he feel the need to put me on the spot? I sat down near the rear of the room and plopped down in the seat. Ciara, one of the only girls I'd considered somewhat of a friend, walked over and stood over the desk.

"Where the hell you been, girl? I've missed you." She reached in to give me a hug.

"You know this school shit isn't for me. I just didn't hear from Mannie this morning so I didn't have anywhere else to go but here."

"You still fucking with him? Girl, I thought you were done with him. Every time I see him he got another bitch in his ride," she said while sitting down next to me.

"Well, we were broken up for a minute; then we got back together," I lied with a straight face. I wasn't about to let this chick know that I was burning up on the inside. I'd always suspected him of cheating and I had even caught him a time or two but I wasn't ready to give him up just yet. He'd done too much for me, hell more than my own father even.

"Oh, okay. Well, what else have you been doing, besides him?" She laughed.

I paused and stared at her for a second wondering why she would even part her lips to ask me about doing my man. Any other bitch would've been slapped, but because she was my girl I gave her a pass. "Getting money; you know me, I stay on the grind."

"Yeah, that's one thing I can say about you, you've always been a go-getter. What's up with your sister? I heard through the grapevine that she was coming back to Philly for good."

"I'd really rather not talk about her, you know . . ."

Saved by the bell: just as I was about to go into how I couldn't care less about Milan or her return to Philly the homeroom bell rang. I quickly gathered my things and walked toward the door. I could hear Ciara's feet shuffling behind me trying to keep up with my fast pace. I wanted to turn around and tell her to get a damn life, but instead I grabbed my headphones out of my bag and quickly put them in my ears hoping she'd get the point.

Talking about my sister was the last thing that I wanted to do. I'd worked hard to come out of her shadow. Regardless of what I did people always wanted to tell me how fucking wonderful she was and how I should look up to her. Man, if they only knew all of the scandalous shit she'd done at my age, they'd have been singing a completely different tune.

As I walked down the hall I felt my pager vibrating in my pocket. I quickly pulled it from the waist of my pants and saw Mannie's number with 911 behind it. Since I was in school I didn't have immediate access to a phone to call him back. I sighed aloud as I regretted coming to school, knowing he'd be pissed if I didn't call him back.

"What's wrong?" Ciara buzzed in my ear like an annoying-ass fly.

"Mannie paged me 911 and I need to call him," I replied.

"Well, go to the counselor and tell her you have to call your mom or something. I use their phone all the time."

For once, Ciara had a bright idea. I nodded my head and said thanks before heading in the direction of the counselor's office. The next period bell was ringing so I knew if I didn't hurry out of the hall I'd have to deal with the hall monitors. I prepped my lie as I opened the office door and walked in with a straight face.

"Can I help you?" the secretary said as soon as I entered.

"Yes, my mother told me to call her once I made it to school. I stayed with my aunt last night and had to catch the bus a long ways so I just wanted to see if I could call her really quick just to let her know that I was okay."

"Sure, just make it quick; the bell just rang." She pointed over to the small room that had a phone on the desk. I walked in and quickly dialed Mannie's number. After a few rings he picked up.

"Hello," he yelled into the receiver.

"Hey it's me."

"What the hell took you so long to call me back? And where are you?" he yelled.

"I'm in school. I had to get to the office to call you back."

"Why are you in school? I expected you over here this morning."

"I didn't hear from you so I thought you were busy."

"I'm coming to get you. Meet me at the corner in fifteen minutes." Click.

Before I could respond I heard the dial tone. I placed the phone back on the receiver and walked back out of the office.

"Were you able to reach your mom?" the secretary asked.

"Yes I did, thank you," I replied as I walked briskly toward the door.

"Don't forget your hall pass," she said, holding out the sheet of orange paper.

"Thanks," I said as I walked over to retrieve it. I flashed her a quick smile before walking out of the office. I looked around the halls before slipping down the back hallways and out of the side door. I ran through the schoolyard and down to the corner where I waited patiently for Mannie to arrive. A few minutes later I could hear the loud vibration of his radio as he whipped around the corner and stopped in front of me. I smiled and walked over to the car. As soon as I was about to grab the handle he took his feet off of the brakes and the car began to move. I stepped back, caught off-guard. He sat inside cracking up as he stopped once again.

"Mannie, stop playing before I get caught out here and they drag my ass back in school." I pouted.

"Aww stop whining like a little kid and get'cha ass in this car. You should've never went to school in the first damn place." He raised his voice.

I obediently got inside the car, straightened my face, and kept quiet. Many times I had been on his bad side and caught a backhand across the face. It took me awhile to learn, but eventually I figured out that Mannie was a sweetheart as long as I did what he said.

"You know you fucking up my money disappearing and shit. I had two clients this morning and your ass was nowhere to be found."

"I'm sorry. I really tried to reach you."

"Yeah, well you'll make it up to me later on but right now I got some shit for you to do."

In other words, he had someone for me to screw. God knows I hated this life, but what else could I do? For the past three months I'd been lying on my back, spread-eagle for stranger after stranger. The worst part of it all was that Mannie didn't give me a penny of what he made.

There was a time when Mannie worshiped the ground that I walked on. I mean, he was my first love and when I fell, I fell hard. I remember the day that we met as if it were yesterday.

I was leaving school with my girl Ciara and a few other chicks laughing and giggling when a black Mercedes pulled up beside us. Of course we stopped, wondering who was sitting behind the luxury car adorned with tinted windows. Ciara was the first one to walk over to the car once the passenger window rolled down. The rest of us just looked on, none of us as bold and outgoing as she was. She was dressed from head to toe in designer gear. She was one of the lucky ones to have parents who could afford it. Me, on the other hand, I was wearing hand-me-downs that my sister had worn when she was my age. Unfortunately, she used to be a tomboy so there was nothing sexy or appealing about my attire.

We all stood anxiously waiting for the result of her approach. We were only about four feet away from the car but because of the loud music we couldn't eavesdrop as well as we'd have liked to. After about two seconds Ciara turned around with the pouty face.

"What's wrong?" I asked as she walked back over to where we were standing.

"He wants you," she replied.

"Me? What do you mean he wants me?" I asked full of confusion.

"He said tell you to come over to the car," she said before shoving me in the direction of his car.

I slowly walked over and bent down into the window. I was immediately mesmerized. He was gorgeous in every sense of the word. He had a smile that could brighten an entire ballroom. His skin was smooth and emitted a glow like it had been airbrushed by a professional photographer. If he wasn't so thugged out, I'd have sworn he was wearing makeup because he was almost too perfect. He smiled after noticing how hard I was staring at him. I didn't know what to say; I was literally tongue-tied.

"What's up, shorty? What's your name?" His voice flowed over the beat like it belonged on the track.

"My name is Shekia," I replied with a slight stutter.

"It's all right, love. I won't bite you, I promise. My name is Mannie. It's nice to meet you, Shekia," he said as he extended his hand to shake mine.

"It's nice to meet you too." I smiled bashfully. If I were a few shades lighter I was positive both of my cheeks would have been apple red right now.

"Well, Shekia, I'd like to see you again if that's possible."

"Really?" I asked. I was still unsure about what he actually saw in me.

"Yes, really. I think you're beautiful. Actually, you're the most beautiful girl I've seen in a long time so I'd be a fool not to want you on my arms."

"Wow, no one's ever told me I was beautiful before," I replied honestly.

"Well, get used to it. Here's my card. Call me later on and I can come scoop you up for a night out." He passed me the card and softly rubbed my hand.

"Okay, I will." I smiled.

"All right, don't stand me up. I want to see you."

"I won't," I replied with a girlish giggle before backing away from the car and waving good-bye. I was stuck both literally and figuratively. I was still standing in the same spot when he sped off and turned the corner. The girls ran up behind me breaking my trance.

"What did he say?" Ciara asked.

"He said call him tonight and gave me this." I showed them the card.

"Girl, you better call him," Ciara yelled.

"I am," I said as I placed the card into my right pocket for safe keeping. I didn't want to show it, but I was beyond excited.

That day would be the start of our relationship or partnership or whatever you'd like to call it. I mean he wined and dined me, showed me all of the finer things. Within two weeks I had almost every designer dress, bag, and shoe you could think of. I'd been to some of the fanciest restaurants and hotels that Philly had to offer. It was like a fairy tale: too good to be true. The irony is how real that statement became. It only took two months for me to find out what Mannie really wanted from me. I wasn't the only girl he'd wined and dined, preparing them for dates. On the outside I felt like the biggest fool on the planet. Here I was happy to show off all of my new gear and tell everyone how Mannie was all mine when, in reality, I was just a piece of property that made cash for him. I was too embarrassed to tell anyone, especially Ciara. I always thought back to that day we met and wished he'd wanted Ciara instead. I figured that he only chose me because I had low self-esteem and Ciara was just too confident. I always hoped I could get out of it, but I didn't know how. Now with my sister coming back in to town I really had to find a way to make her believe that Mannie was my man and not my pimp. She definitely didn't need another reason to look down on me for my naïveté.

It wasn't long before we were pulling up to Mannie's spot where the client was waiting. I looked in the mirror and applied some red lipstick, fixed my hair, and put on mascara. Quietly, I got out of the car and went to work as I did every day.

Chapter Three

Milan

With Change Comes Responsibility

Damn! I just walked away from the love of my life to possibly end up alone. What the hell was I thinking? Wait, what am I talking about? I'm young, extremely smart, and no one can deny the fact that I am exceptionally beautiful. I will have the men in Philly eating out of my hand. I laughed aloud as I thought about how silly I was even thinking that I would be lonely. Shit, who could resist my fine ass?

See, I was what some would call conceited, and I could honestly admit that I didn't care what people said since they could never call me stupid, ugly, or broke, all of which I knew I was far from. I was the chick everyone loved to hate, and I sopped it up like gravy with a buttermilk biscuit.

After boarding the Amtrak train heading to Philly, I decided not to look back, and instead stare my future in the face. The ride was surprisingly quiet causing my mind to wander freely, creating different scenarios for my arrival. It had been five years since the day that my mother shipped me off to Georgia to live with my father. I had spent at least five hours preparing my look for today since I needed to make a good impression. I wanted them to see how well I had turned out despite what everyone

thought. I was doing better than any of their asses, and I
had to put myself on display to make them feel like shit
for ever doubting me in the first place.

For most of the ride I sat looking out of the window
at the scenery, not because I was really interested in
sightseeing, but mainly because I was trying to avoid
looking at the pervert sitting across from me. If there was
one thing that I hated it was a man who didn't even try to
hide the fact that he was practically getting a hard-on just
from looking at you. If I wasn't shitty sharp in my Donna
Karan suit I would have cussed his ass out, but I couldn't
afford to screw up my look by fighting his stupid ass.

I had never really been lucky when it came to men.
I'd been in love a few times, but each time I ended up
dropping their sorry asses. I couldn't understand why
a woman with all of the qualities I possessed ended up
single. I always attributed it to the fact that most men
can't handle being with a woman who is more successful
than them, and so far I always had more than they did.
I had just broken up with my boyfriend of four years
because of this, and though I was hurt when I walked
away, I did love him; but being in Philly, many miles away
from him, would have to be the medicine I needed to get
my mind right.

My mother and sister were supposed to pick me up
from the Thirtieth Street train station at six o'clock p.m.,
and it was almost five o'clock. After hours of staring out
of the window I finally dozed off. I was awakened at 6:05
when we were pulling into the station. The pervert got
up and tapped me on the shoulder to let me know we'd
arrived. I knew his concern was just a way for him to cop
a feel, but I politely said, "Thanks," instead of saying what
I really wanted to say.

After picking up my luggage from the holding area
at the end of the car I headed out to the street to look

for them. I took a deep breath once I spotted them, and headed over. I didn't know where to begin so I tried to be serious, and not laugh out loud or smile when I realized that they didn't even recognize me.

"What you don't remember me or something?" I said placing one hand on my hip.

My mother looked at me as if she was ready to cry, and by her reaction I didn't know whether she was happy to see me. She laughed softly before grabbing a hold of my hand and smiling. "You look so beautiful. I guess going to Georgia worked out for the best huh?"

Hugging her I said, "I guess it did!" I turned to my sister, who was standing off to the side with a shocked expression on her face as if she'd just seen a ghost. I knew that I looked good, but damn, I wasn't expecting the reaction that I got from either one of them.

"What's up, little sis? I'm so glad to see you. Where's my hug, or are you too grown for that?" I laughed while reaching out my arms to embrace her. "I really missed you," I said honestly, because our relationship had changed drastically since I moved away. Our once "two peas in a pod" closeness had turned into two peas in separate casings. I planned on getting things back on track, and upgrade her to my level. I could tell by glancing at her that fashion wasn't something she was interested in, but I was going to fix that one way or another.

The drive to the house seemed especially long, and maybe it was because I was so anxious to get there. I missed the old neighborhood, and the few friends I'd had. I couldn't wait to see how each of them turned out in comparison to me. I looked at my sister as she sat in the passenger seat reading a *Vibe* magazine, and she definitely looked a whole lot different than what I remembered. She was now about five feet five, maybe a size six at the most. Her hair was pulled back into a ponytail and her clothes were pretty average.

As we pulled up in front of the house all of my old memories came back, including sneaking boys in the house at night when my mother worked extra shifts at the hospital, which was part of the reason she shipped my ass away. I wondered who all of the people were in front of the house. I felt like a movie star on a red carpet at an awards ceremony as all eyes were glued to me. I recognized two of the faces, which were those of my best friends Danell and Tramaine. I instantly felt warm and the coldness that I assumed I would feel when I arrived had melted away.

Danell was like a sister to me, and I loved her just as if she were a blood relative. We had our problems every now and then growing up, but there had never been a problem big enough to break our bond. As teens we spent a lot of time together, and the mixing of our personalities kept us in trouble. Danell had the rebellious attitude, and, me, all I cared about were my looks and getting guys to want me. Danell's mother passed away when we were both twelve, and she was never the same after that. She still had her dad, but he couldn't fill the void that came from losing her mother. I could remember the day that she lost her virginity; she said that she only did it to piss her father off. Anything that got a rise out of her father seemed to turn her on. I never understood her reasoning. I thought everything she did was ridiculous, and that she would pay for it in the long run. After I went away we still remained close through letters, and phone calls. She still looked the same to me. Tall and thin, she had a short haircut now that to me was all wrong for the shape of her face. She wasn't dressed all that spectacular either, just simply wearing a pair of blue jeans and a white tank top, an outfit I wouldn't be caught dead in.

Tramaine on the other hand was my blood relative, my first cousin. She was like my shadow when we were growing up. She always strived to do whatever it was I did, and rock whatever gear I chose to wear. She succeeded, and ultimately became another version of me. She was dressed in a pastel-colored maxi dress with pastel-colored Gucci sandals. Her hair was past her shoulders, wrapped with a little bend and an even part down the middle. One thing about Tramaine was that she always wanted the best, and by the way that she looked I could tell that she was able to get just that.

As I hugged them both, suddenly the rest of the faces became familiar. My aunts, uncles, and other members of my extended family had also come out for my welcome home party. I was flattered, and extremely excited about catching up with them.

I mingled after eating, and learned a lot about how things had changed since I'd left. The once-quiet neighborhood was now flooded with drug dealers, and fiends. I was disgusted knowing that things had gotten so out of hand. I knew that living in Philly again was going to be a totally different experience than what I had in Atlanta. I vowed to make the best of it despite the obstacles that would probably be thrown my way. After grabbing a glass of wine I sat down in the living room with Danell and Tramaine to talk. I looked at them both, and smiled, as I was happy about the way all three of us turned out. I felt that it was pretty impressive for three girls from the ghetto.

"So, how was it down there? The only thing I hear about Atlanta is that it's full of strip clubs, rappers, and gays," Danell said before taking a sip of her drink. It was funny that even after all of these years she still held her drink in her mouth a few seconds before swallowing. I used to tease her all the time about that when we were younger.

"That's a shallow description," I said before laughing. "I mean yeah, you will find those things in ATL, but that's not all that's there. There are tons of things to do, and the weather is much nicer of course. I didn't really get to hit the club scene too often though, because I was always working or going to school. I honestly believe that going to live with my father was the best thing for me. Who knows what the hell I would have gotten into had I stayed here?"

Tramaine smiled. "Yeah, I heard you got a degree in fashion, so you a big shot now!" She giggled.

"Yeah, it was easy to get, too. Fashion is my life. I mean look at me; I look like I just stepped off the page of an *Elle* magazine advertisement. Who could ask for anything better? I get to travel often, and not to mention all of the money I get paid for doing what I love." I smiled.

"That's cool. I still want to get into the fashion business. I still draw every now and then," Tramaine replied while talking about her love of fashion. Even at the age of twelve she was an excellent fashion illustrator so I knew she could have only improved over the years.

"Why don't you go to school? It only takes a year for a certificate. That's enough to at least get you started," I said. I wondered why she'd never pursued it when she loved fashion just as much if not more than I did.

"That's it?" she asked, obviously shocked by the short length of time.

"Yeah, that's it. I'm thinking about opening a store. I just have to get my head together first, you know, get settled down here."

"So where are you going to work now?" Danell asked.

"The company I work for transferred me down here so I'll go back to work on Monday. But enough about me; I need some juice. What the hell's been going on down here?" I was anxious to hear more about all that I'd missed.

Danell put a huge grin on her face and replied, "Girl, it's been crazy. I got a man now. His name is Melik. You might remember him; he went to Strawberry Mansion. Him and his crew always came to the basketball games. We've been together for almost two years now."

Voluntarily I gave up some information about my broken relationship. "I have a man in Georgia. Well, I had a man, but once I told him I was moving here, he came up with some bullshit-ass excuse about not being into long-distance relationships. I know that it was all a lie since he travels all the time. Our relationship was practically long distance already. He comes to Philly all the damn time so you know he's running game."

"Men are so full of it, shit, even my man Tyron. If it weren't for all the money he throws my way I would have left his cheating ass a long time ago. I know that he be messing around with other chicks, but he gives me so much. I'm at the mall every other day spending his money, and all they're getting is dick. I just wish he showed me a little more love; even though I'm used to it I'm tired," Tramaine chimed in.

"Well, why don't you leave him; it's not worth it!" I blurted.

"Shit it's worth it to me. I don't have a good job where I can afford to buy the things I want like you. Sometimes you have to put up with bullshit to get to the diamonds, honey."

"Well, soon when I get the store together you won't have to worry about money. It ain't no reason why you should have to be with someone who is not loving you completely. It's too many men out here!" I preached.

"I know that but there ain't many men out here who will give me the things he does. I've never met a man like him. I know he loves me, because he wouldn't do half of what he's done if he didn't."

"Girl, you'll learn you can't be staying with a cheating man; they will never stop, and it takes more energy than it's worth," I responded honestly while Danell looked as if she wasn't really interested in our conversation any longer.

"We're going out clubbing tonight; you coming with us?" she interrupted.

"What time are y'all leaving?" I asked.

"Probably around ten," Danell replied.

"Well, come back and get me. I'll be dressed," I said.

"All right!" Danell said before getting up to leave.

"I'm glad that you're home, Milan," Tramaine said before giving me a hug.

After walking them to the door I headed up to my sister's room. I softly knocked on the door, and waited a few seconds before turning the handle. She was spread out across the bed with a pair of headphones on humming the words to the tune she was listening to. Her eyes were closed so it took a few seconds before she realized that I was even in the room. Embarrassed she quickly sat up, and removed her headphones.

"What's up?" she asked while setting her iPod down on her bedside table.

"I just wanted to talk to you before I headed out of here tonight," I said as I moved farther into the room.

"Cool, what's going on?" she asked.

"What's been going on with you? You're growing up on me, looking just like Mom!" I said, nudging her on the shoulder. "How's school?"

"It's good. I'm going to a prom this year!" she responded, excited.

I could remember going to my prom and how excited I was. She reminded me so much of myself. "Whose prom is it?" I asked since I knew that she wasn't old enough to be going on her own.

"My boyfriend, Mannie," she responded confidently.

"Mannie? How long have you been with him?" I asked.

Smiling she said, "Since last year. He's real good to me."

"Well, I hope so. It seems like everyone has a man but me!" I said jokingly. "I'm going to pick up my car tomorrow so maybe I'll pick you up from school, and we can go shopping or something."

"Okay." She smiled.

I got up and headed toward the door. I took one more look at her before leaving. I missed her, and I missed being there. I was glad to be back, and I was going to make sure that our relationship was tighter than ever.

I went into my old room, which surprisingly was the same way that I left it, even down to the sheets. I sat down on the bed, and smiled as I looked around. *Home sweet home,* I thought.

After showering I looked through my bags to find an outfit to wear. I settled on a black-and-white color-blocked dress, and black stiletto heels. I looked delectable, and there wasn't any denying that. The men would be drooling once I walked through the club with my video vixen body. I hoped that the two of them would look almost as good so I wouldn't feel guilty about stealing all of the attention.

After they arrived we headed down Center City in Tramaine's white Nissan Maxima, a car that suited her well. It wasn't too expensive but not too cheap either. Tramaine always treaded somewhere in between extravagant and average. When we arrived the line was outrageously long. I was glad that it moved quickly, but I felt like an ass for waiting when the bouncer told me we could have paid an extra ten dollars to walk right in. After entering the club Danell began dancing immediately. Tramaine and I went over to the bar to get a drink since I needed a buzz before I could dance. As I sat and ordered my Long Island iced tea a guy came over, and sat next to me.

"You know, you have the prettiest face I've seen all night," he said, smiling.

"Oh, really?" I replied. I wasn't convinced of his authenticity since I knew that he'd probably spat that same game to a ton of women in the club before reaching me.

"Really. I know that it wasn't all that original, but it's the truth. Look around, and you can see for yourself," he said, pointing at the random women on the dance floor.

"Yeah, you're right," I said, laughing since I was the finest face in there. I thought I would have at least had a little competition.

"My name is Mike. It's nice to meet you . . ." he said, extending his hand.

"Milan," I replied while placing my hand in his.

He slowly bent down, and planted a kiss on the backside of it. "Wow, that's a hell of a name, and Milan is a beautiful place so it definitely fits." He laughed. "Would you like to dance?"

Though I wasn't really in the mood to dance yet, I said yes. There was something about him that caught my attention. We danced for about a half hour before I took a break. He was definitely a nice-looking guy, and his Drakkar Noir cologne was turning me on. After he ordered me another drink we found a small table to sit down and talk.

"So, what part of the city are you from?" he asked, trying to pry information out of me.

"Well, originally I'm from North Philly, but I just came back today from Georgia."

"How long were you down there?"

"Five years."

"Oh, wow. So, Miss Milan, do you have a man?" he asked getting to the point.

"No, I don't."

"Well, I'm not really looking for a relationship myself, and I'm pretty sure that you're not since you just came back, but I am looking for a friend. So if you wouldn't mind me calling you sometime I would love to have your phone number."

"That's fine with me," I said before retrieving a business card from my purse.

"Well, I have to work early tomorrow, but I'm sure glad that I stayed a little while longer because I almost missed you," he said with a warming smile.

"Well, in that case I'm glad you did too. I'll be waiting for your call, okay?"

"Okay," he replied with a grin.

After he walked away I got up from the table to find Tramaine, who was still sitting at the bar.

"So who was that fine-ass guy you were talking to?" she asked, taking a sip of her drink.

"His name was Mike."

"Okay, playa! Got a number already!" She laughed.

"Girl, I'm just about ready to go. I'm exhausted. Have you seen Danell?"

"No, I haven't, but she won't be hard to find, I'm sure. That girl gets dance fever when she drinks," she said.

Once we located her she said she would catch up with us later since she had a ride home. Tramaine was cool with that since that was one less stop she would have to make. I, on the other hand, was a little annoyed since I believed that if you came to the club with your friends you needed to leave with them. Have the nigga pick you up after you make sure your girls get home safely.

"I wonder who's taking her home," I said aloud.

"Probably her other man. He doesn't live here. I think she said he's from Baltimore. Sometimes she meets him at the club when he's in town, and they hang out," Tramaine responded.

"I thought that she loooooovved Melik so much!"

"That's what she says, but she loves Amir, too!"

"Amir? That's the same name as the guy I broke up with in Georgia."

"For real? Ain't that a coincidence?"

Yeah, that really is, I thought as we headed to her car.

Overall the day had gone well, but I knew with change comes responsibility, and I was ready for whatever was thrown my way. It wasn't long before we were pulling up in front of my mom's house, and after the long day I was beat. I went straight up to my room, put on a T-shirt, and climbed into bed.

Chapter Four

Sapphire

Love and War

"Babe, what time are you coming home?" I asked. I had a night planned that was sure to blow his mind. Enzo and I had been going strong for the past two months and I couldn't have been any happier. I hadn't quite moved in yet but I was hoping that I could whip it on him and get more than just a drawer in his dresser.

"I'm not sure yet. I got a couple of things to take care of," he replied.

"Well, should I wait up?" I asked, hoping he'd say yes.

"Naw, you can do you. I probably won't be in before two or three."

"Damn, Enzo, when are we going to have some quality time? You go through all the trouble to get me and then you act as if you don't even want to see me."

"Listen, I'm not about to argue wit' you. I'm handling fucking business. Matter of fact, you can go the fuck home so I don't have to see your ass when I do decide to come in," he yelled before hanging up the phone.

I sat there with the phone in my hand looking at it to make sure that he had really hung up. That certainly wasn't the effect that I was going for. I had spent all day getting the bedroom decorated with roses, and bought the champagne and some sexy-ass lingerie for a night of passion. Enzo was so unpredictable. He could be in a great mood and in an instant turn into a raging animal. I always felt as if I was walking on eggshells, unsure of what I could say or do. I wanted to think that he loved me but, to be perfectly honest, I wasn't sure. After a few minutes of pondering I decided that I wasn't going to let all of my hard work go to waste. I was just going to sit up and wait for him.

As the hours passed on the clock I grew sleepier. It wasn't long before I had dozed off. I woke up when I heard his keys in the door. I also heard giggling and a female tone. I jumped up and quickly made my way to the living room where I walked smack into Enzo and his female companion. Clearly he'd picked up a random bitch from the strip club.

"What the fuck is going on, Enzo?" I yelled with one hand placed on my hip and my other hand waving in the air.

"What are you still doing here? I thought I told you to go home," he replied, clearly intoxicated.

"So you can bring another bitch in here? Really, Enzo? I'm not going any-fucking-where! I'm your woman and this little groupie bitch can turn right the fuck around," I yelled.

I was furious. I could feel my temperature rising with each second. I'd never been so disrespected in my life. Here I'd changed my entire life for this man and he'd changed nothing.

"Who are you calling a groupie bitch?" the female yelled.

"Oh, I'm sorry, maybe slut is more fitting. I don't give a fuck who or what you are. What your aren't going to do is fuck my man in the bed that I sleep in, so you can take your fake-ass Gucci bag and wack-ass weave and get the fuck out of here."

I was fuming and the whole time Enzo stood there with a smirk on his face. I wanted to slap the shit out of him but I knew that wouldn't make things any better.

"Are you going to stand there and let her talk to me like that?" the female questioned. "You know what? Fuck this. I'm out." She turned around and headed toward the door. She slammed the door as she left and you could hear her cursing on her way down the front steps.

I stood there holding back the tears as Enzo shook his head and walked into the kitchen. He grabbed a Corona out of the refrigerator and popped the top before taking a sip. I stood at the entrance of the kitchen in disbelief.

"So you don't have anything to say?" I asked, waiting for him to spit a lie, yell, or do anything besides standing quiet. I wanted to know what he was thinking and what his excuse was for bringing another bitch to the house.

"Naw, I don't have nothing to say." He continued to drink his beer.

"So you're not even going to try to defend yourself?"

"For what? What are you gonna do? Leave? We both know that shit ain't gonna happen." He laughed.

I stood there feeling lower than low. He was right. I wasn't going anywhere. I didn't know what to say or what to do at this point. I'd lost my job because I chose him. I'd even alienated myself from my family devoting all my time to him. Enzo once told me that he would never let me go and I believed that the moment I would attempt to leave he'd make my life hell. I wanted to cry but I fought back the tears. Enzo walked over toward me, and looked at the lingerie that I had on. I'd completely forgotten that I was wearing it when I stormed into the living room.

"Nice outfit." He smiled before brushing up against me and grabbing a handful of my ass cheek. He set his beer down on the counter and grabbed a hold of my chin before kissing me forcefully. I didn't resist since that would only piss him off. I wasn't in the mood to be yelled at or, even worse, popped upside the head as he'd done before in similar situations.

After a few moments of tonguing me down he paused to speak and retrieve his beer from the counter. "Today's lesson is this: when I tell you to do something do it. If you'd gone home like I said, you wouldn't have been here to see me with another bitch. Keep that shit in mind next time you decide to disobey me. Now meet me up in the bedroom in a minute. I need my dick sucked." He exited the kitchen and walked up the stairs.

I stood there and waited a minute before going upstairs. He was right; it was my fault. I should've listened and now I had to do whatever I could to get on his good side again. I walked up the stairs slowly, making sure I gave him enough time to get comfortable. When I walked into the room he was naked, sitting on the edge of the bed, stroking his dick. He was hard as a rock. Even though I was still a little upset I was turned on. Enzo was sexy as hell even when he wasn't being so nice.

"Get over here," he said in a mellow tone.

Without a word I walked over and assumed the position on my knees. I used one hand to pull it downward and quickly stuck it in my mouth. I grabbed his balls with my left hand while using my right hand to jerk his shaft in a circular motion, never moving my lips from the head. I sucked on the tip of his dick like it was a green apple Jolly Rancher, and I loved Jolly Ranchers. With my eyes wide open I stared up at him. If there was one thing that could turn his attitude around it was good head. I released it from my mouth every so often, making that popping sound that would send any man wild. Then I gathered some spit in my mouth and hovered over it, letting the spit drip from my lips onto his dick and down the shaft onto my hand, which continued to jerk it up and down.

"Damn, bitch, I'm about to bust all over that pretty face of yours. You know that right?" He moaned.

With his dick still in my mouth I nodded yes. I continued satisfying my man the best way that I knew how. Without warning he stood up and turned my back toward the bed. He pushed my head back onto the edge of the bed where his ass had been planted throughout this sexual expedition. With his hands on the bed he stuck his dick in my mouth and began to ram it back toward my throat. Since I was known to deep throat some of the largest dicks known to man, I handled it with ease, not gagging once.

"Suck this dick, bitch. Yeah, just like that, make that shit sloppy," he said breathlessly.

I sat there sucking as hard as I could and within a few minutes he pulled his dick from my mouth and came all over my face and breasts.

"Woo, damn, babe, that shit got my legs shaking. That was just what a nigga needed," he said before walking over to the bed and plopping down on his side.

I got up and went into the bathroom to clean myself up and stared into the mirror. I hoped that I'd done enough to satisfy him. I never wanted to witness him with another woman again. After I cleaned myself up I headed into the bedroom, hoping for a late night snuggle but he was stretched out, asleep. I decided to just climb in bed softly and not disturb him. I lay there staring at him, knowing that this was just another bump in the road. I didn't expect any relationship to be perfect and I'd prepared myself for the worst. Soon I drifted off to sleep feeling confident that the next day we'd be fine. Even though all of the romantic aphrodisiacs I laid out went ignored, I thought the head I gave him would make up for my failure to obey his command.

Boy was I wrong. Enzo woke up the next morning with an attitude. He barely spoke to me and after getting dressed he headed for the door.

"I need all these roses and shit cleaned up, and tonight stay home, all right?" he said before heading downstairs and leaving the house.

I wanted to scream. I thought for sure that we'd be fine the next day. I had to map out a strategy. I couldn't sit and let my relationship go down the drain. I'd walked out on my job because he asked me to. I was used to bringing home no less than $1,000 a night and now I was depending on him. I couldn't even buy deodorant unless he gave me the money to get it. Love is a strange thing because it will have you doing things that you never imagined you'd do. It would also have you going to war for a relationship that most people would think you were foolish for staying in. The good thing was I never cared about what other people thought. I was a bad bitch and I could make up my own damn mind. With Enzo was where I wanted to be and there wasn't anything that would make me feel otherwise.

Chapter Five

Shekia

One-minute Man

"Girl, you know exactly what to do. That nigga Mannie wasn't lying," he said aloud as I went up and down on his miniature-sized version of a real dick.

Anything this small couldn't even be classified as the real thing. If the size weren't bad enough the smell was even worse. His balls smelled like he'd been playing basketball for five straight hours. I was holding back vomit as I hoped he would hurry up and bust a nut so this could be over with. I reached under and grabbed his balls, massaging them just enough to make him explode. Soon, I could feel the heat of his cum underneath the condom. I sat up and used my hand to wipe the excess saliva from the sides of my mouth.

"Girl, you suck dick like no other. Damn." He shook his head and stuffed his dick inside of his funky-ass drawers.

I got up from the floor and made my way to the chair, awaiting his exit. As soon as he left the room I ran into the bathroom and turned on the water. The cheap motel wasn't equipped with much so I always carried my own toothpaste, mouthwash, and soap. The bathroom was filthy. Mannie paid the owner well not to have anyone enter the room. This included cleaning staff. Often, he'd make me and his other girls clean the room ourselves. I took the mouthwash and swished it around in my mouth for at least three minutes, then grabbed a washcloth and vigorously washed my face. I wanted to be rid of his body odor. As I stood in the mirror with tears running down my face I just prayed that this would all soon be over with. I quickly got my emotions under control once I heard banging on the bathroom door.

"Hurry up now. I got another one for you," Mannie yelled.

"Okay, I'll be out in a minute," I replied.

"A minute is all you have. I'm sending him in."

"Okay." I finished freshening myself up, and reapplied makeup to my face to make myself as pretty as possible. After a minute I opened the door to find a guy sitting on the edge of the bed talking on a cell phone.

"All right, I'm gonna hit you back in a few," he said before hanging up.

I walked over to the bed and sat down next to him. Mannie always told me to let the customer lead and let me know what they wanted from me. So I sat patiently to see what he wanted.

"What's your name?" he asked.

"My name is Alyssa," I replied, giving him the name that Mannie told me to use.

"I mean your real name. I know that's not it."

"I can't tell you my real name."

"The guy I paid said you'd do whatever I wanted you to do. All I asked was your name."

"I'm really sorry, but I have to follow the rules or he'll hurt me."

"Hurt you?"

"Yes, hurt me. Now how else can I help you? Please tell me what it is before he comes busting in here."

"So you're telling me this isn't what you want to do?"

He was asking too many questions. I didn't even know what to say. I just wanted to finish this job so Mannie could take me home.

"Please just let me do my job," I replied.

"Listen, I don't want anyone to do something that they don't want to do. This shit isn't something I need to do; it's just something that I do. I can get tons of bitches but they all expect a relationship. This gets me satisfied without all the extra bullshit, if you know what I mean."

"Okay, well, how can I satisfy you?" I asked.

"You're not hearing me. If you don't want to do this then you don't have to."

"No, you don't understand. If you don't leave here with a smile on your face it will end really bad for me."

"I'm gonna make sure that doesn't happen, okay? Now calm down. I would never go out there and tell him anything but what he wants to hear. I don't know why but as soon as I saw you come out of that bathroom I felt that I needed to get to know you. It would be simple to just fuck you or let you suck my dick, but I felt you needed help. How old are you anyway?"

"I'm almost seventeen," I replied honestly.

"Wow, you should be in school somewhere, definitely not out here doing this. I can help you if you really want to get out."

"He'd never let me go."

"Oh, I could make it happen. Trust me."

"Why would I trust you? I don't even know you. You could be just as bad as him."

"That's true, you don't know me, but, really, what could be worse than this?"

I sat quietly.

"Listen, my name is Enzo. Now, can you tell me your real name?"

"My name is Shekia."

"Okay, that's a start. Look, I'm going to give you my number and I want you to call me when you leave here. I promise I'll help you out of this situation if that's what you really want." He passed me a sheet of paper with his number on it.

"Thank you."

"Don't thank me yet; you have to make the first step. I'll be waiting for your call though." He got up from the bed and began to walk to the door.

"Wait, you can't leave yet. What are you going to tell him?" I was afraid that he'd know something was up if he left so soon.

"I'll tell him I'm a minute man." He laughed. "Look, don't worry, he said you were his best girl so I'll convince him that it was that good. I only need a little time." He grabbed the handle of the door before smiling and leaving.

I tucked the number into my bra and ran into the bathroom to smudge my lipstick. I couldn't look too perfect. Mannie came into the room about two minutes later and called me out of the bathroom. I was scared shitless. I thought I was caught for sure. I slowly opened the door to find him standing there with a smile.

"You did good today. So good I'm going to take you home early. You must've did a hell of a job on that last one 'cause he paid me an extra tip. Shit, I need you to keep up the good work." He bent down and kissed me on the forehead. "Get your stuff, let's go."

I quickly grabbed my things and walked out behind him toward his car. I was quiet as usual, trying to stay on his good side. I didn't want him to change his mind about taking me home early.

The ride home seemed to take forever. I was just anxious to get home and call Enzo to see if he'd really help me. Once we pulled up in front of the house I grabbed my bag from the back seat and reached for the door handle to exit. He stopped me.

"Don't try to disappear on me tomorrow. I need you working early in the morning so be waiting for me on the corner."

"Okay," I replied without looking back at him. I got out of the car and briskly walked to the door and into the house. Once I closed it I exhaled and made my way up to my room. I wasn't up there five minutes before my sister came knocking.

"Hey, how was school?" she asked, poking her head into the room.

"Umm, nothing exciting. A pretty typical day," I said, trying to conceal the clothing that I had just removed. I hadn't made it to the hamper before she came. I didn't need her questioning me about what I'd worn.

"Oh, okay. I thought we could sit up and have girl talk. I want to catch up." She smiled.

"You know, Milan, I have a test to study for and then I'm going to take it down. I'm really tired. Yesterday was a long day and I really didn't get much sleep."

"Oh, okay, I understand; maybe another night. Well, good luck with your test. I'm just in the other room if you want to talk or need my help with anything."

"Okay," I said, wanting to shove her out of the door. Since when did she give a fuck about how my day in school was or helping me? She was faker than a six dollar bill and I wasn't buying that shit.

I found the number that Enzo had given to me and dialed it. The phone continued to ring unanswered. Once the answering machine picked up I just hung up. I didn't feel comfortable leaving a message. *Maybe he hasn't made it home yet,* I thought.

I tried again every hour on the hour until I fell to sleep. When I woke up the next morning I was pissed.

I was angry that he had sold me a pipe dream. He'd made me believe that he was really going to help me and he'd proved that it was all a crock of shit. He wasn't any different than any other man I'd met, and I felt foolish for believing that what he told me was the real thing.

I got up and got dressed feeling defeated. Here I thought the previous night would somehow be my last working night. I didn't have any other choice but to work or else I'd suffer the wrath of Mannie. After I got dressed, I left as if I was going to school the same as I did every day, and walked to our meeting spot. I waited patiently for Mannie on the corner just as I was told. Like clockwork, he was there just as he said he would be. I got inside and said good morning.

"You look nice today," he said with a smile before driving off.

"Thanks," I replied while glancing out of the window. I was mentally preparing myself for the day ahead with a silent prayer. I always prayed that God would remove him from my life somehow. I didn't know when and I didn't know how but I trusted that my prayers wouldn't go unanswered. As we approached his spot, as usual he asked, "Are you ready to work?"

"As ready as I'll ever be," I replied. *God help me.*

Chapter Six

Milan

Gonna Miss My Love

Shit! I thought. It was already nine o'clock and I had so much to do. I already felt like I was behind. I had to unpack, get my car, and go shopping for new clothes. I hadn't bothered to bring much with me since the weather in Philly was much different than back in GA.

After getting dressed I called Danell and told her I was on my way over, since she was going to drive me to pick up my car. As I headed out of the door I noticed a guy who looked so familiar coming out of the house next door. *Damn he's fine,* I thought as I tried not to stare. His name was on the tip of my tongue but I decided to walk on by instead of being embarrassed by calling him the wrong name. As I walked by I felt him grab my arm.

"I know that's not tomboy Milan?"

I laughed once I realized who it was. "Devon, what's up?" I yelled while giving him a huge bear hug. His body felt good next to mine but I attributed that to the fact that I hadn't been next to a man in a few weeks.

"Nothing much. I see you're not a tomboy anymore. The grown and sexy look fits you much better." He smiled as he looked me up and down.

"Thanks," I said, blushing. "You don't look so bad yourself," I admitted with a slip of the tongue. *Damn, I don't want him to think I've been checking him out.*

"So are you living back in Philly now?"

"Yeah, I finally got my job to transfer me."

He smiled. "So what do you do? Because I see you're rocking all expensive gear from head to toe. Either it pays really well or you have a damn good man!"

"I'm a fashion buyer," I said confidently. "It's the job, trust me, definitely not a good man. I haven't been so lucky to find one of those."

We both laughed.

"So what have you been up to, still playing basketball?" I asked with a smile.

"When I get a chance but the boy is getting too old for that shit now." He laughed. "I cut hair up Germantown though. I live up that way."

"Well, it was good seeing you. I have to go pick up my car but I'm back so I'll be seeing you around," I said, smiling and leaning in for one more hug before I walked away.

"Yeah, it was great seeing you too," he replied.

As I walked away I switched my ass even harder because I was certain that he was looking. I couldn't believe the difference five years made because he was definitely not that fine back in the day. Devon and I used to be best friends growing up. We were like family and since I was a tomboy I fit right in with him and his friends. I missed him for months after I left, and I was kicking myself now that I'd seen him because I didn't keep in contact with him. As I turned the corner Danell was coming my way, probably pissed that I had her waiting so long.

"What took you so long?"

"I'm sorry, I ran into Devon. Girl, he is so fucking fine! You should have warned me about him!"

"I know, he is fine. You know he own a barbershop up G-town?"

"No, he told me that he cuts hair but he didn't say he owned the shop."

"Oh, yeah, he's got plenty of dough and he don't have any kids either," she said loudly.

"I still can't believe how good he looks!" I was still stuck.

"Well, get over it, girl, because he does look that damn good!"

We both laughed.

As we headed up the expressway all I could think about was Devon. I wanted him but I couldn't let him know that and seem desperate. Eventually he would come on to me; they all did.

After we sat in the car dealership for almost three hours catching up on all the neighborhood drama I was clear to take my car. I drove away in a brand new Infiniti J30, black with all-black interior. The leather on the seats formed to my ass when I sat in it and I was ready to show it off. I followed Danell home to drop her father's car off and then we headed over to pick Shekia up from school. She was shocked when I pulled up in the new car. I guessed she didn't realize how well off I really was. We hit the mall and I was ready to splurge. I noticed that in each store Shekia wasn't really looking around. I thought that it was kind of strange. I mean what woman could be surrounded by a sea of clothing and not look around?

With curiosity I asked, "Shekia, what's wrong, you don't like shopping or something?"

"This stuff is too expensive," she replied.

"Well, get whatever you want, I'll pay for it."

"Are you sure?"

Annoyed, I replied, "Girl, go ahead and get something before I change my mind."

At her age I would have wrecked the mall if someone told me to get what I wanted. It took a little too much convincing for her to grab an outfit; I could see that there was one thing we didn't have in common.

We spent at least five hours at the mall and I ended up spending much more than I expected. While dropping Danell off we decided to meet up to go out again that night. Tramaine said she wouldn't be able to make it since she planned an evening with her man. I took a nap before waking up to get dressed and was fully energized ready for a night of fun. I was excited about returning to the club especially now that I had my new car and gear. I felt more like myself and ready to shine on every chick who thought she could touch me. I'd give them the "bitch, please" look and keep on walking.

We arrived at the club around eleven o'clock and headed straight to the bar. After ordering we sat there and sipped our drinks until a tall, light-skinned guy came over and grabbed my attention. Danell headed out to the floor as I stood there engrossed in conversation with the fair-skinned stranger.

"So is this your first time here?" he asked, leaning over so that I could hear him over the loud music.

"No, it's my second."

"I saw you when you pulled up outside. You must have a nigga wit' money to be pushing that."

"Actually, I don't. I bought it myself," I replied, annoyed that he insinuated I needed a man in order to drive a nice car. Shit. I had all the money. The niggas I was with in the past ain't have shit!

"Damn, I'm sorry, Miss . . ." He placed his hand on his chest and took a few steps back.

"Milan, the name is Milan," I replied sharply.

"Well, excuse me, Miss Milan, but around here the only chicks pushing whips like that fuck with hustlers."

"Well, I don't fit that mold, sorry. I actually have a college degree and a job," I replied, still annoyed with the whole conversation.

"Well, Miss Educated, do you think a nice brotha like me could have your number so I could call you sometime?"

I had to think about it for a second. Although his rap was tired and he annoyed the hell out of me, he was cute. He wasn't nearly as cute as Devon's fine ass but I could give him a chance.

"Yeah, I'll give you my business card," I said as I passed him the card and smiled.

"Okay. I'll make sure I give you a call."

"Okay." I smiled as he walked away. I checked out his build and he was definitely working with something. I loved a man who had strong shoulders and arms so he could throw me around in bed.

After finishing my drink I headed out to the dance floor and danced for a while. The DJ was spinning all of the hottest tracks and the atmosphere mixed with the alcohol had me going. I hadn't seen Danell since she walked away from the bar so I began looking for her. I noticed her in a conversation with a guy who looked extremely familiar, but under the dim lighting I couldn't really see his face. I didn't interrupt, but as soon as he walked away I approached her.

"Hey, girl, who was that guy you were talking to? He looked familiar."

"Oh, that's Amir, my side joint. He doesn't live here in Philly; he come down here one week out of every month and we get together. He's coming right back. I'll introduce you to him."

We stood there for a few minutes waiting for him to come back, and as he got closer to where we were standing the steam began rising from my head. *This lying muthafucker!*

"Amir, I want you to meet my best friend. Milan, meet Amir," she said, placing her hand on his chest.

My heart dropped down to my stomach as I looked into his eyes. The man who just told me a couple weeks ago that he couldn't handle long-distance relationships was screwing with my best friend all this time. I knew that it was a bunch of bullshit. I pondered if I should tell her but I figured that it would open up a can of drama I wasn't in the mood to deal with. If I ever saw him again after this I would definitely give him a piece of my mind. A few seconds later, I snapped out of my daydream.

"Hi, it's nice to meet you," I said, giving him a fake-ass smile since him even being near me at this moment was making my skin crawl.

"It's nice to meet you too." He extended his hand for me to shake it. I quickly shook his hand and let go. I couldn't wait to find a sink so I could wash my hand.

"Milan, are you ready to go?" Danell asked me after noticing the change in my appearance. "You look tired," she said.

I was trying to cover up the fact that I was angry enough to jump over her and whoop his ass in this club for standing here disrespecting me.

"Yeah, I am a little tired." I held my composure.

"Okay, baby, I'm gonna go but if you are still coming by later call me," she said to Amir as she leaned in to kiss him.

It made me sick to my stomach and the worst thing was how he kept a straight face the whole time. I should have slapped him for kissing her in front of me but I didn't want to look like an asshole in this club.

"You ladies be careful going home. It was nice meeting you, Milan."

"Likewise," I sharply replied.

We headed out of the club and I didn't even turn to see if he watched us walk away. I was eager to drop her off so that I wouldn't be subjected to hearing anything more about Amir.

I was still in shock as I waved good-bye to her and drove away. After parking at home I sat in the car for a few seconds to get my mind right before going in. I didn't want my mother to instantly notice that I was upset. After gathering my thoughts and putting another fake-ass smile on my face I stepped out of the car. Devon was coming out of his mother's house as I was headed across the street.

"I see you're riding in style. You're getting money now for sure," Devon said, laughing.

Blushing, I replied, "Something like that."

Just looking at him made me weak in the knees as I tried hard not to let on to him that I was mesmerized.

"Hey, I never found out why you left. What happened? If you don't mind me asking."

"I was out of control, don't you remember? My mom couldn't handle me anymore so she shipped me off."

"Well, I can see that it worked out for the best," he said, looking me up and down.

"So how long have you been out of your mother's house?" I asked, trying to take my attention off of how good he looked.

"Two years, but I'm still here every day." He smiled.

I began laughing and he soon joined in. "Still a momma's boy?"

"You know it!" he admitted.

"Do you remember when we used to stay out here all night while you tried to teach me how to box?"

"Yeah, I would always let you win," he said, putting his hands up, reminiscing.

"Yeah, whatever," I replied, nudging him on the shoulder.

"For real, I just wanted to make you feel good," he said, getting serious.

"Well, in that case I guess I could say thank you."

We both laughed as we pictured it. It's funny how you forget the good times as you get older, and how, as your life changes, you no longer think about how those things make you who you are.

"Well, since you're here every day, I guess I'll see you tomorrow," I said as I headed toward my house.

"I guess you will," he replied.

As I walked away I smiled from ear to ear. I wanted him and I was sure that he knew it. I mean, who wouldn't want a man as fine as him?

Before I walked into the house a car pulled up in front of the door and double-parked. I stopped for a few seconds when I noticed my sister sitting in the passenger seat. I wouldn't have thought anything of it if it weren't two o'clock in the morning.

"Where are you coming from?" I asked as I blocked the door.

Abruptly she replied, "From my man's house."

"Does Mom know where you were?"

"No, and she doesn't have to."

"If it happens again she will. I'll make sure of it," I said, hoping that she wouldn't do it again. I knew that road all too well and the trouble that it would get you into.

"No problem," she said as she brushed past me to get in the door.

After going in she went straight up to her room and didn't say another word to me. I didn't care that she was upset since I was only looking out for her. I knew all about staying out all night and having sex with a man. I did it and ended up pregnant at fifteen but I thank my mother for forcing me to get that abortion because my life would be so much different now if she hadn't.

I wasn't going to stress myself that night since I had calmly avoided the ultimate drama less than an hour earlier. I went upstairs to take a shower and as the water ran over my body I exhaled to release some of the stress. Things certainly were turning out a lot different than I expected. The vision of a warm welcome had been lukewarm. My sister had changed drastically. The baby sister I'd left and had been close to was long gone. I'd hoped we could've picked up where we'd left off. I wasn't giving up on our relationship but I wasn't going to push her too hard either. More upsetting was the lying bastard Amir who I'd devoted myself to only to be slapped in the face. I'd never been so disrespected but I'd get over it. I was too fly to cry over spilled milk; needless to say Amir was no longer relevant.

After my shower I plopped down on the bed so hard you heard an echo in the room. I felt myself drifting to sleep shortly after my head hit the pillow. It had been another very long day. . . .

Chapter Seven

Sapphire

Love On Top

"Keep your eyes closed, no peeking," Enzo said as he guided me toward our destination.

I was excited to see what he had planned. Surprisingly, Enzo had been on his best behavior since the last incident with the other chick. I couldn't have asked for anything better. This was the man I fell head over heels for, and I was truly happy to see him return.

"I'm not looking, just don't let me bust my ass, okay?" I replied with my hands covering my eyes. I hated surprises, but I didn't want to seem ungrateful so I played along.

We walked forward a few more steps, and finally he told me it was okay to open my eyes. I opened them one at a time, nervous about what would be standing in front of me.

"Baby, you didn't," I screamed as he dangled a set of keys in front of me. There I was staring at my brand new Mercedes 420E. The sight was beautiful. Though I was used to getting money, and doing things on my own, I would've never purchased an expensive car like this. I was fine with my Honda Accord.

"I can't have my woman driving around in no Honda, fuck that, you have to ride in style. Check the key ring; there's more where that came from."

I looked down at the keys in the palm of my hand, and noticed a house key. I looked over at him wondering what it was for since I already had a key to his house. "What is this for?"

"That there is the key to your brand new condo right on Penn's Landing over the water."

My jaw dropped. Was he serious? Where did my real boyfriend go? Because this man who stood next to me was almost too good to be true. I screamed and jumped on him, damn near causing him to fall to the ground.

"I can't believe you did all of this for me," I said, wrapping my arms around him. I had the biggest smile on my face. I was sure he could see every one of my teeth.

"Why is that? You're my woman and I needed to show you that I appreciate you. I know I'm not always the easiest person to deal with, and the fact that you stick around even when I'm the biggest asshole on the planet says a lot. It tells me that you really love me and you will be there to hold me down when I need you." He leaned in to kiss me.

"Wow," I replied. I couldn't think of anything else to say. I was honestly speechless at that moment.

"Well, let's get in. I want to take you over to the new spot," he said as he walked over to the car and got in the passenger seat.

I looked down at the keys and smiled before walking over to the car. On the drive over to the condo we were pretty quiet besides him telling me the directions. I'd always seen the buildings along Penn's Landing and wondered what they looked like inside; now I was finally going to get my answer.

We drove into the parking lot where he pointed me toward the designated parking space for my unit. Even the parking lot was upscale. I became more anxious with each step toward the elevator and even more anxious as we walked down the hall.

"You ready?" he asked.

"Of course." I smiled.

He grabbed the keys from my hand and opened the door to the most amazing living space I'd ever seen with my own two eyes. Immediately you were greeted with a living room, which was filled with tons of plush furniture. An oversized cream-colored leather sofa caught my attention first. Beneath it was a brown and cream rug and right on top sat an all-glass coffee table with a large exotic flower centerpiece. The curtains matched the colors in the flowers, something I thought only a woman would have thought of. I hadn't even gone through the entire apartment and already I had a million questions. It was almost too good to be true. I didn't want to get too excited and get let down once he decided that I didn't deserve it anymore.

"Who decorated this?" I asked.

"Does it matter?" he snapped. I could immediately tell that I'd annoyed him.

"No, baby, it doesn't matter. It's just amazing. I've never seen anything like this," I said before walking over to him and hugging him. He quickly pushed me away.

"You always know how to fuck up a mood. I got some shit to handle so I got Rock downstairs waiting for me. Do what you please; the spot is yours. I'll hit you up later," he said before walking toward the door.

"Baby, I'm sorry," I said as tears began to develop in my tear ducts. He exited the apartment without another word. I sat down on the sofa and looked around. I couldn't even enjoy it after the way he'd left. I wanted to call him and apologize and promise him that I would never question him again. It was another mistake on the long list of them that I'd made throughout my relationship with him. After a few seconds of silence there was a knock on the door. I smiled and hurried to the door expecting it to be Enzo coming back. I swung open the door to find a female standing patiently.

"Can I help you?" I asked.

"Is Tina here? I thought I heard Enzo," she replied.

"Yeah, you heard Enzo but there ain't no Tina here. I'm Sapphire, can I help you?"

"Naw, is Enzo still here?"

"No, he isn't. Now, if it's nothing that I can do for you I'd appreciate if you backed up from my door," I said loudly.

"Look, I'm not trying to start no shit. I just needed something and I thought Tina was here. Could you tell E that Jessica came by please?"

"Jessica? That's your name?" I walked closer to her. I wanted her to feel my presence and know that I wasn't the one to fuck with. "Listen, Enzo is my man. I don't give a damn who Tina is or who you are for that matter. What I do know is I'm not delivering no fucking message, and the next time you knock on my damn door, you'll be greeted with my fist. Now back up, bitch!" I yelled.

She began to laugh as she backed away from the door. "Well, Sapphire, you might want to do some research on your so-called man because you're not the first woman he's brought here, nor will you be the last. He loves saving hoes." She continued to laugh as she walked down the hall toward her unit.

It was just like a jealous bitch to try to steal your happiness. I wasn't falling for that shit. I closed my door, and decided that I would spend the rest of the evening getting to know my new place. At first I was tempted to call Enzo and let him know about the surprise visitor, but quickly changed my mind. I walked over to the window and looked out onto the water. I could have never imagined that I'd be where I was at that point.

Shit, growing up was hard for me. I lived with my grandmom for most of my younger years until she grew tired of me sneaking out at night fucking different boys. My mother had never been around. I was always told how much I reminded her of a situation that she wanted to forget. When my mother was only fifteen she gave birth to her one and only child, who was also her sister. Yes, I was the product of incest. My father/grandfather raped my mother's young virgin pussy, and knocked her up. Back then it wasn't acceptable to get an abortion so she was forced to go through with the pregnancy. My Aunt Sylvia told me that my mother tried on numerous occasions to force a miscarriage. She would punch herself in the stomach, drink bottles of alcohol; she even made herself fall down a flight of stairs only to end up with a broken leg. She refused to hold me the day that I was born and once they brought me home she never fed me, held me, or changed any of my diapers. When I was four months old she ran away with an older boyfriend, and never came back. She passed away when I was twelve from a drug overdose. I didn't even attend the funeral. Even though she was my mother, I didn't shed a tear because I truly believed that she would have never shed any for me.

I started stripping when I was seventeen because I was dead-ass broke with nowhere to go. My grandmother had kicked me out, my Aunt Sylvia had five kids of her own, and I didn't have a man at the time. Working at the club taught me one thing and that was just how much a woman's body was worth. To make more money I perfected my skill. I always believed that you should give your profession your all whether it was working at the supermarket or on a pole.

My relationship with Enzo was just the same. I wanted to give it my all but it was extremely hard at times. I felt like everything I did made him angry. I was still staring out the window when there was another knock at the door. *I know this bitch isn't knocking again,* I thought. I bent down and took off my heels because I was sure to deliver the ass whipping that'd I promised. I stomped over to the door and quickly swung it open.

There was huge teddy bear tied to three balloons staring at me. The delivery guy peeked around the teddy bear before speaking. "I have a delivery for you, miss," the young Spanish delivery guy spoke.

I grabbed the teddy bear and placed it on the floor to sign for the delivery.

"Enjoy," he said with a huge smile and waved good-bye.

I closed the door and looked at the gift. I felt horrible about doubting my man. There he'd done all of this for me and I'd messed it all up. I pulled the attached card from the teddy bear's neck and opened it. It read:

> *Tina,*
> *Here is your weekly gift. Hug him tight when I'm not around.*
> *Love you,*
> *E*

I read the card at least three times trying to make sure that I was reading it correctly. I immediately thought about the unexpected visitor Jessica, and what she'd said. Who the fuck was Tina and why is there a package being delivered to her here? All sorts of things flowed through my mind. Rage filled every inch of my body even down to my fingertips. I ripped up the card and threw it down on the floor next to the teddy bear and grabbed my purse and keys off of the table. I was going to go give him a piece of my mind. I'd be damned if I'd be made to look like a fool. Fuck love; this meant war!

Chapter Eight

Shekia

Sometimes I Rhyme Slow

I was miserable, both sick and depressed. I honestly thought about committing suicide, but what would that solve? Obviously, that would kill my mother and I wouldn't want to hurt her in that way. I was tired of Mannie using me and not reaping any benefits. Granted, I hated what I did, but a few dollars in my pocket would make it a little easier to deal with. I walked slowly with my books in my hand dreading my day. I didn't know how much more of this I could take. As I walked toward the corner to wait for Mannie a white car pulled up and stopped right in front of me.

"I've been looking all over for you," Enzo yelled from the driver's seat.

"Really? I find that hard to believe," I said with my mouth twisted. Fool me once shame on you, fool me twice shame on me. I wasn't going to fall for his game twice.

"Why is that? I told you to call me, and you didn't," he said, getting out of the car and walking over to where I was standing.

I was nervous because I knew Mannie would be showing up soon. I didn't need any drama. I was already stressed enough. "I called you numerous times; every hour on the hour as a matter of fact."

"Well, why didn't you leave a message?"

"A message? Why? I don't know your situation and the last thing that I need is an angry girlfriend playing on my phone." I shook my head before I said, "And, furthermore, why did you tell me to call if you weren't going to be available?"

"Listen, some shit came up but it really wasn't my intention to be unavailable. Why you keep looking around? Scared somebody watching you?"

"No, Mannie is on his way to meet me so I don't want him to catch me talking to you."

"This nigga really has you shook. Well, listen, if you want to roll with me you can," he said, pointing to his car.

"And then what?"

"And then I got'chu just like I said I would," he replied while rubbing his hand on his chin.

"What about Mannie?"

"What about him? Listen, I know you don't know me, but trust me, he does. Mannie doesn't want any problems."

I stood there thinking about what he said and looked down at my watch knowing Mannie would pull up any minute. If there was one thing you could bet on when it came to Mannie it was that he was always on time.

I stood there for a second wondering what to do next. My heart was telling me to jump in the car and throw caution to the wind but my mind was saying stand still and do as I was told. Mannie was scary and I could hear his voice as if he were screaming in my ear at that very moment. I wanted a change but I wasn't sure if this was the way to get it. Mannie could be extremely abusive both mentally and physically. There were numerous occasions when my body was bruised from his attacks. He kept his hits to my body so my face was always spared. There was even one incident where he'd pointed a gun to my head and promised me that he'd shoot me if I didn't do what he said. So many questions but as I looked down at my watch I knew that any decision I made had to happen quickly. I decided to follow my heart and believe that Enzo could be just the change I needed.

"He'll be here any minute so can we just leave?" I asked, glancing back and forth between Enzo and the corner.

"All right then, let's roll," he said as he opened up the passenger side door.

I hurried inside, hoping that we would drive off before Mannie pulled around the corner. I breathed a sigh of relief once we were off the block.

"Are you okay?" he asked.

"Yes, I'm okay," I lied. I wasn't okay. I was scared shitless. "So where are you taking me?"

"Where do you want to go?"

"I don't know, anywhere that he can't find me."

"Well, how about this: we can go to grab you something to eat and then we can hang out at one of my spots; then I can drop you off at home after school's out. Is that cool?"

"Yes, that's . . ." I paused when my pager began to go off. It was Mannie.

"Is that him?" he asked.

"Yes, it's him."

"Just ignore it. Don't even worry about that clown," he replied.

We drove to a soul food restaurant and I sat patiently in the car as he ran in and returned with two bags of food. Mannie continued to page me so eventually I got sick of the beeping and turned it off. I was almost tempted to run to a pay phone and call him. I thought maybe I could lie and say I was kidnapped or something thinking that would get me off the hook.

"He still paging?" Enzo asked once he sat down in the car.

"I turned it off."

The rest of the ride I remained quiet. So many thoughts running through my mind I couldn't figure out what I needed to do. When I was younger I wanted so much more for myself. I always wanted to show my sister that I could do better than her in every sense of the word. If she knew what I'd become I was sure she wouldn't waste time rubbing it in my face. I knew I had to do better; I had to figure out a way to get my life back on track. I looked over at Enzo who was totally engrossed in the lyrics of "Sometimes I Rhyme Slow" by Nice & Smooth. Ironically, the verse was speaking about a girl fighting with substance abuse. No, I wasn't addicted to drugs but I was addicted to a man. Addicted to the hope that he would somehow return to the man I met and fell in love with. Just like the song, I had a savior, a knight in shining armor but here I doubted his authenticity. I didn't want to end up like the song: right back where I started. I wanted to trust him; hell, I needed to. I didn't have any other options at the moment.

Soon we were pulling up in front of an apartment complex. My stomach was in knots. I was almost afraid to get out of the car fearing that someone would notice me and tell Mannie where I was. I sat still even after he exited the car. He walked a few steps toward the door before realizing that I hadn't gotten out yet. He walked over to the passenger side door and opened it.

"What's wrong?" he asked, holding the two bags in one hand. "Look, no one is going to fuck wit'chu, I promise." He extended his hand.

I took a deep breath and got out of the car to follow him. I was walking so fast I was damn near on his back. I just wanted to hurry up inside. He shook his head at my actions. If he only knew the magnitude of what I'd gone though with Mannie he'd understand my actions completely. We entered the small apartment that was most certainly a bachelor's pad. It was filled with luxury furniture and textiles, mostly black with accents of white. I'd never been in a place so nice. I looked around in amazement as I slowly made my way into the living room.

"This is really nice," I blurted with wide eyes.

"Thanks. Make yourself at home," he said, setting the bags down on the dining table. Just then his phone started ringing. "Excuse me," he said as he walked over to the table and grabbed the cordless phone off the base. "Speak," he said into the receiver while walking into the other room.

I took a seat on the sofa as I waited for him to reemerge from the back. A second or two later I heard him yelling.

"Who the fuck is you questioning? Do I ask you about every nigga you fucked before me?" he screamed.

From the sound of it I could tell that it must've been a female, possibly his woman. I wanted to get up and eavesdrop a little better but I decided to stay put.

"Listen, I got company. I'll talk to you later." He was on his way back out to the living room. "So where were we?" he said before placing the phone back down. The phone immediately began to ring again. "I'm sorry, one second," he said, picking it back up. "Speak," he yelled. "Listen, I said I'll talk to you later. Now stop calling my fucking phone," he yelled before slamming the phone back down.

"Girl problems?" I asked.

"Naw, that ain't shit. You ready to eat?" He quickly changed the subject.

"Sure," I replied.

"Good, 'cause I'm starving. I'd hate to eat in your face." He laughed. He motioned for me to walk over to the table. After taking everything out of the bags we both sat down to eat.

"I really want to thank you for this. I know you didn't have to."

"No need to thank me, I told you that already."

"I mean what made you decide to help me? You could've just fucked me and left."

"I don't know. You reminded me a little bit of my little sister. I felt obligated to help you."

"How old is your little sister?"

"Well, she was seventeen when she died from a drug overdose," he replied before taking a spoonful of his food.

"Oh, I'm so sorry to hear that," I replied honestly.

"Thanks. Yeah, she got hooked up with the wrong nigga and shit went downhill after that, you know. I wouldn't be able to forgive myself if I didn't help you."

At that moment I understood and believed that he was truly genuine.

"Well, I appreciate you." I smiled.

"It's all good. I want to know more about you." He smiled, looking me in the eye.

Bashfully I looked down; I was extremely intimidated by him. I mean he had his shit together and I was just a big mess. "There isn't much to tell," I finally looked back up and replied.

"It has to be."

"Well, I have one older sister, who I can't stand. I live with my mother and my father lives in Atlanta. I haven't been to school in months, I'm failing everything, and I suck dick for a living. That about sums it up."

He sat there for a minute before speaking. "Well, we're going to change that. Make life more exciting."

"I'd like that."

"Cool."

Just then there was a knock at the door. He took a sip of his soda before walking over to the door. "Who is it?"

"It's the police. We need to speak to you regarding a missing person," a voice said from the other side.

He looked at me then looked at the door. I immediately thought they were looking for me so I got up and ran to the rear of the apartment. I heard him opening the door.

"How can I help you, Officers?" he said.

"I'm Officer James and this is my partner, Officer Brown. We're investigating a missing person, one Tina Waller. Are you familiar with who she is?"

"Yeah, I know who she is; she's my son's mother. What do you mean she's missing?" he asked.

"Her mother reported her missing. Said she didn't pick up her son and hasn't been able to reach her for two days."

"Huh?" he asked. "I haven't spoken to her. Are you sure? She would never disappear without her son."

"That's precisely what her mother said, which is why we came to you."

"You think I have something to do with her disappearing? That's the mother of my child. I would never hurt her. I really need to see my son, sir. I don't know where she is but I'm surely going to do my best to locate her. Do you have any contact information for me to reach you? I really need to get to my son to make sure he's cool."

"Yeah, here's my card. We'll be in contact but make sure you contact us if you hear anything."

"I will, thanks," he replied. Afterward, I heard the door close, followed by footsteps. "Shekia," he called out.

"Hey, is everything okay?" I asked.

"Naw. Look, you can stay here. I have to run and see about my son. I'm sorry to leave but I promise I'll be back to take you home tonight, okay?" He grabbed his keys off the table.

"No problem. Take care of what you need to."

"Cool. My pager number is next to the phone if anything's up. Be back soon."

"Okay."

Once he left I turned on the TV and relaxed. *I could get used to living like this,* I thought. I took my shoes off and sat back on the sofa. I was comfortable and soon I was drifting off to sleep.

Chapter Nine

Milan

I've Been There a Time or Two

The following morning I woke up too late to catch my sister, so I figured I would talk to her once she got out of school. As I fixed breakfast all I could think of was Amir and it showed because I damn near burnt my pancakes. I still couldn't get over the fact that he cheated on me, and worst of all with her. I sat down to eat when my phone rang. I answered it after a few rings and the deep voice on the other end surprised me; it was my father.

"Hey, Dad!" I said excitedly.

"How's everything going?" he asked as I took a bite of my food.

"Everything is okay. I got my car!"

"Yeah? What did you get?"

"An Infiniti."

"That's nice, baby. So how are your mother and sister?"

"Mom is good but I think Shekia is about to get into some trouble."

"Why do you think that?" he asked, concerned.

"Because I know how I was and she's following the same path. I'm just a little worried about her," I said honestly.

"Well, talk to her; maybe you can get through to her if you explain it that way."

"Well, that's what I'm hoping to do."

"Well, good luck, baby. I'm glad that you made it okay. I just wanted to hear your voice. I have to go so I'll call you later."

"Okay, I love you!" I said before hanging up. I missed my dad already and it hadn't been long since the last time I'd seen him. He had always been there for me and even though he was strict as a drill sergeant I thanked him for it.

After I finished my food I went upstairs to get dressed. I wanted to get my nails done and get a pedicure. After the evening I had I needed some pampering so that I could relax my mind as much as possible. I put on Fendi from head to toe and I must say I was the shit! I decided I would drive to Danell's house to see if she wanted to go with me.

As I parked I looked over and saw Amir leaving her house, and walking over to his car. I rolled down my widow and yelled across the street.

"New York, huh," I said sarcastically.

"Milan, what's up?" he asked, probably surprised to have run into me again.

"You know I believed that you loved me. The entire time it was all a lie," I said angrily.

"No, it's not even what you think. Me and her are really just friends," he replied.

"Don't give me that bullshit, Amir, she told me about you."

"She couldn't have told you much because there isn't much to tell."

"Well, she sure doesn't have to tell me that you stayed here last night because I can see that shit for myself!"

"Milan—"

"If you were going to cheat you could have found someone who looks better than me!"

"See, that's your problem, Milan: you're too stuck on yourself. I love you, don't get me wrong, but if you didn't spend so much time worrying about your looks I wouldn't be here," he shot back.

"You know what, don't worry about me. I'll be just fine. She can have you."

"Believe it or not, I stopped worrying about you a long time ago. I know that you'll be fine. It was fun while it lasted," he replied sarcastically.

I rolled up the window and got out just in enough time so he could see what he was missing. Shit, he was the one going to miss me, and all of my loving; it definitely wouldn't be the other way around. Danell was my girl, but she had nothing on me. How could he have wanted a broke-ass chick with no goals? I had the world at my fingertips and that's what he wanted? I quickly changed my mind about asking her to go with me since I wasn't in the mood to hear about her having sex with him. So, I got back in my car and drove away. I went to Tramaine's house instead.

"Hey, girl, what's up?" she said as she opened the door.

"I have something to tell you but I'm on my way to the nail salon; do you want to ride with me?"

"I'm not dressed."

"Girl, you look fine, we are going to be in the car, and these bitches don't have shit on you. You could be rocking a plastic bag and still shit on them."

"All right," she agreed before putting on her sneakers and grabbing her bag.

As soon as we got in the car I began talking to her about the situation with Danell and Amir. "You know the guy Amir Danell mess with?"

"Yeah, what about him?"

"That's my Amir from Georgia!"

"What? How do you know for sure?" she asked, shocked by the accusation.

"We went to the club last night and he was there. She introduced him to me and that muthafucker acted like he didn't even know me. "

"For real, what did you do?"

"I didn't do anything last night. I didn't want to make a scene in the club but today I drove over to her house and he was coming out of the door."

"What did he say? Girl, 'cause my ass probably would have gotten locked up for whipping his ass." She continued quizzing me for information.

"I told him that I couldn't believe him. He actually stood there and said they were just friends. I ain't no fool! I'm sure he doesn't fuck and spend the night with his 'friends.'"

"Girl, how is he going to cheat on you with her of all people? She ain't a supermodel you know," she said, laughing.

"I know." I laughed. "She is my best friend and all, but I don't even feel comfortable being around her at this point."

"Well, you know I don't care for her too much anyway. You don't need her; that's what you have me for."

"I know, girl!"

We went to the nail salon and, after leaving there, went on a little shopping spree. Anytime I had a lot on my mind shopping would help me relax. I didn't really need anything new, but I ended up spending $1,000 anyway. After dropping Tramaine off at home I went to go fill out applications for apartments. I didn't plan on staying at my mom's long. By the time I filled out five applications it was two o'clock. I drove to my sister's school to pick her up. I waited outside until three and she never came out. I decided to go inside and talk to someone in the office. I wasn't surprised when they said she hadn't been to school. So when I picked her up the other day she came around just in time for me to get her. I had a few choice words for her once I caught up to her. When I pulled up at home, Devon was on his mother's step.

"It's funny how we keep meeting like this."

"If I didn't know any better I'd think you were stalking me." I laughed.

"I'm definitely not a stalker." He joined me in laughter.

"Have you seen my sister today?"

"No."

"I don't know what's up with her. She hasn't been to school all week and she's been sneaking out at night saying she was at her man's house, whoever the hell he is."

"Look, I know it's not my place, but your little sister is a working girl, if you get my drift."

"What? What does that mean? I know you're not saying she's a prostitute!"

"That's exactly what I'm saying. That's where she goes all the time. She works for some nigga named Mannie."

"I can't believe this. I don't know why she would do that. She acts like she doesn't have any money and she's a hooker? What the hell is she doing it for if she's not getting paid?" I asked, disturbed.

"I don't know, but I got to get back to work. You know, you should stop by the shop sometime," he said as he stood up from the step.

"Maybe I will," I said softly.

"I hope so," he said as he walked toward his car, which was parked near the corner.

As I walked toward the house I thought about his facial expressions and I knew that he probably had that beautiful smile on his face. His smile could definitely brighten up your day even when it wasn't going so well. I went into the house and noticed that my mother wasn't home yet so I just sat on the living room sofa and collected my thoughts. I was stuck with the thought that my little sister was out there fucking men for money. Or was it really for money? There had to be other reasons since she obviously didn't have any money.

With the overload of thoughts I got a headache so I lay down to take a nap. I woke up to the smell of fried chicken. My mother was home and I hadn't even heard her come in. I went into the kitchen to say hello.

"So did you talk to your sister today?" she asked.

"No. I went to the school to pick her up and they said she hasn't been there in a good while."

Calmly she responded, "I'm not surprised; she's been doing that the whole school year. I don't know what has gotten into her, but it needs to stop before I put her fast ass out in the street!"

"I heard some crazy things about her today. I don't know if they are true so I won't tell you exactly what they are. But I really need to talk to her before things really get crazy."

"You know, I remember when you used to put me through the same trouble, hanging out all night, getting into fights and getting pregnant."

"I know and I'm really thankful that you sent me to Georgia because I probably would be in the streets doing nothing with myself. You and Dad helped me a lot."

"Well, hopefully you can talk some sense into her."

"I'll see what I can do." I hugged her before going outside to sit on the steps. The sky was beautiful as I looked up thinking about Shekia. I wanted to sit there and wait for her, but I knew that she wouldn't be back anytime soon. I needed someone to talk to so I drove back out to Tramaine's house.

"Back so soon, what's up?" she asked, surprised to see me.

"I know. I have a lot on my mind and I needed to vent."

"Well, come in," she said, stepping back so that I could enter the apartment. "What's up?"

"Devon told me that Shekia is a prostitute."

"What?" she yelled. "Did he really say that? I mean is that even possible? She's so young!" she replied, just as shocked as I was when he told me.

"I know, but I believe him. I mean he doesn't have a reason to lie."

"That's true, but why would she have to? Her man has plenty of money from what I hear."

"I don't know. I want to talk to her but I don't know where she is."

"Hopefully she'll listen. I know you really care about her. Hell, I do too, you know. I definitely want to do what I can to help."

"Thanks, girl. It's just depressing. I expected things to be much different when I came back. I've almost been blindsided with all of this."

"Everything will be okay, I'm sure of it. But enough of the depressing talk; it's ruining my mood." She laughed, obviously trying to lighten up the conversation. "So where are you going tonight?"

"I don't know."

"You want to go out to a bar or something?"

"No, not really. I wish I had a man so I could get some dick!" I laughed.

"Well, you need to find one. Don't be worrying about Amir because you're too pretty for that. If he wants a chickenhead over you, it's his loss," she said, laughing.

"I'm not worrying about him. That's old news now," I said, flagging her. "And besides, you know who is looking damn good to me right now though?"

"Who?" she asked.

"Devon!"

"Girl, tell me something new. He got plenty of cash and no kids either. If he's as good in bed as he looks, he's definitely a keeper!" she said with a giggle and slapping me a high five.

"I know that's right," I said, agreeing. "He asked me to stop by his shop so I told him that I might do that."

"Girl, you better not pass him up."

"I'm not, trust me. Matter fact, I'm going over there right now," I said, gaining the confidence I needed to approach him.

"You go 'head, girl! And if you change your mind about tonight, give me a call."

"Okay," I said as I got up to leave the apartment.

I drove up to the block where Devon's barbershop was located to see what he was up to, and hopefully let on to him without being obvious that I wanted to get with him. When I finally found it I hesitated. I knew that if I went in, there would be no turning back. I sat in the car for a minute, watching a group of children running up and down the street and a few old men sitting in chairs outside laughing at each other's jokes. These were the good times that I missed. The part of Georgia where I lived you didn't see too much of this. I watched and smiled until I gained the confidence to get out and walk in. As soon as I entered the crowded shop every guy in there stared at me. Devon noticed me and immediately stopped talking.

"Hey, what's up? You decided to stop by?"

"Yeah. I was waiting for my sister to come home but I knew that it wouldn't be anytime soon," I said, walking over to the spot where he was standing.

"Let's go in the back to the office," he said, pointing in the direction of the hall that led to his office.

As we walked down the hall I pictured us walking to the bedroom to make love. I knew that we would be the perfect match, and I just hoped that he knew it too. Maybe I was jumping the gun, almost like a young girl with her first crush. There was just something about being around Devon that made everything better, almost as if having him in my life at this moment was meant to be. I instantly thought about my previous relationships and I couldn't think of one whom I could honestly consider a friend. I thought the friendship that Devon and I had could only be icing on the cake.

The office was exceptionally nice to be in a barbershop, with plush carpet and leather furniture. There was black art on each wall with a huge floor-model TV. I knew that he didn't want me to know how well off he was. That was why he never told me the shop was his. It was sweet to be protective but I had my own cash and plenty of it. One thing I wasn't or would ever be was a gold digger. I sat down on the couch and continued looking around the room.

"This is a nice office," I said, smiling.

"It serves the purpose. So what's up? Are you going to get with me or what?" he asked abruptly.

I definitely wasn't expecting that. It took me a second to respond since I was a little shocked by the question. "It depends," I said playfully.

"Depends on what?"

"On how much you want me," I said, now that I had the upper hand. Prior to this moment I was sure he didn't know that I was feeling him as more than a friend, so now I wanted to see exactly how far I could take it.

"Oh, believe me, I want you a hell of a lot!" He laughed.

"Well, all you have to do is prove how much. You can't always believe what someone's mouth says. Actions speak so much louder than words."

"Well, let me start by taking you out so I can work on that. Trust me, I don't have a problem with showing and proving."

"No problem. When do you want to take me out?"

"Shit, I'd take you out right now if I wasn't working, but how about tomorrow?"

"That's cool. Here's my number. Just call me when you're ready."

"Will do!"

I walked out of the office and tried not to smile since I didn't want everyone to see how happy I was. I strutted out of there like a model on a runway at a fashion show. All of the men were on me for sure but Devon was the only one on my mind.

I got in the car and drove away. As I got closer to home I snapped out of heaven and quickly came back to reality. I still had to talk to Shekia and I knew that it probably wouldn't go easy.

I turned the corner and noticed a large crowd in front of our door. I didn't have any idea what it was about but I knew that it couldn't be good whatever it was. I parked the car and quickly got out. Pushing my way through the circle of people I found my sister in the middle fighting another female. I didn't know who she was and at that point I didn't really care; I just wanted to break it up before someone really got hurt. Once I got closer to them I noticed my mother already unsuccessfully trying to pull them apart. For an older woman she was pretty strong but she obviously was no match for either of them. I wasn't about to have my mom knocked down or injured because of some stupid quarrel. I reached in and got her loose; then my mother quickly pulled her into the house.

"All right, show's over!" I said loudly.

The crowd began to move away slowly. I turned to go inside of the house, ignoring the obscenities the other girl was spewing.

"You see what I'm talking about? I'm too old for this shit!" my mother yelled after I closed the door and walked into the living room. She was standing there, pacing and rubbing her arm, which I assumed had been hurt in the struggle.

"Are you okay, Mom?" I went over and looked at her arm. She pulled it away from me and continued to walk back and forth, making tracks in the carpet. "Where is she?" I asked.

"She's upstairs," she yelled.

I walked up the steps furious and pounded on her door. "What?" she yelled angrily as she swung open the door.

"So what was that all about?" I asked.

"She tried to say I had sex with her boyfriend." She walked away from the door and stood on the side of her bed with both arms crossed.

"Well, did you?"

"Not yet," she replied.

"Not yet?" I asked, confused.

"He and I are friends. He looks out for me but I love him and as soon as I let him know exactly how I feel sex is sure to follow."

"Shekia, what has gotten into you? Are you trying to give Mom a heart attack? 'Cause if so I'm here to tell you that shit isn't happening."

"Really? What are you going to do about it, Milan? Huh? Nobody's scared of you. I'm not that same little twelve-year-old walking in your shadow anymore."

"You don't have to be scared of me, Shekia, and the bottom line is you'll regret all of this shit later. I heard you were out there selling pussy; is there any truth to that?" I yelled.

"I used to but not anymore. Anyway, what's your point?"

"Well, if you were a prostitute why don't you have any money? Obviously you weren't that good at it," I spat.

"Because I have things to do, and what I do with my money is none of your damn business. I don't need you coming in here trying to act like my mother. One mother is enough!" she said, raising her voice.

"Excuse me! I was just trying to help if you haven't noticed."

"Well, thanks but no thanks. I don't need help from a conceited bitch who thinks she knows everything. You don't give a damn about me. All you care about is you."

"You know what, Shekia, forget it. I hope that you learn your lesson. I'm going to show you what 'only caring about me' really looks like! You will most certainly need me before I need your ass, for sure," I yelled in a rage. I wasn't going to sit there and argue with her any longer. She was obviously angry for some reason unknown to me, and it was times like these when you'd say things you'll regret later, so it was best for me to just walk away.

"Don't let the door hit you on the ass on the way out," she yelled.

I didn't even respond to the last comment she made. At that moment I felt like wrapping my hands around her throat and choking her. I knew she was still hyped up after the fight but she still had no excuse for treating me as if I had done something wrong. She was trying to grow up too fast, and five years ago that was me. I was the same hard-head who thought I knew it all. You couldn't tell me my shit didn't stink. I couldn't care less what anyone's opinion of me was. I didn't have a problem telling anyone including my mother where they could shove their opinions.

Thinking you are in love will have you doing some strange things. It was clear that this Mannie wasn't the best thing for her and obviously things were going to get worse before they actually got better. I could remember my first love, Tylee. Man, I chased him for months until he finally gave me a chance. I loved him with all of my heart; hell, I loved his dirty drawers back then. Ironically, it wasn't until he got me pregnant and disappeared that I realized he was never worthy of me, my body, and certainly not my love. My mother was all that I had after that and felt terrible about the things I did and the way I treated her. After all of the wrong I did, I couldn't understand Shekia, since my mother would break her neck to get her anything that she needed. The attitude that she was giving me let me know that she was hurting inside and yearning for something she wasn't getting. Something was going on that she didn't want us to know about. Instead of pushing the issue I decided to just back off. I didn't want to screw our relationship up more than it already was and I didn't want to bust her in the face for being disrespectful either. I knew she'd need me eventually.

Chapter Ten

Sapphire

Hate On Her

"So, girl, what's been up? Ever since you got with Enzo a bitch's been missing in action." Jannie laughed.

Jannie was a bartender at the Velvet Rope, the club that I used to dance at. Saying I was missing in action was an understatement, because Enzo consumed all of my attention. I'd fallen completely off the map. Most women wouldn't understand how I could even be with a man like him but the things that most people saw as disrespect, I saw as love. The way I saw it, he only got angry because he cared; otherwise, it would amount to wasted energy. Jannie was always supportive of my choices even if she didn't quite agree. I had to say she was more like a sister to me than a friend.

"I know he takes up all of my time but you know I miss you." I smiled.

"Whatever," she said with her lip twisted.

"Well, what's been going on at the club?"

"Girl, you know that chick Eliza you had the fight with? Well, somebody ran up on her and threw acid in her face. Shit melted all her damn skin."

"What?" I asked in shock.

"Yes. They said she almost died, but she's in like an induced coma. Shit, I'd rather die than be fucked up like that," she said honestly.

"Damn, even though I don't like her scandalous ass I wouldn't wish that shit on my worst enemy."

"Right. They said they think it was a female who did it. Probably some pissed off girlfriend or something. You know she was always sleeping with somebody's man."

"True. Well, karma is a bitch."

"It sure is; but enough about that. Let's go eat and finish catching up. I'm hungrier than a hostage right now." She laughed, quickly changing the subject.

I was actually relieved because it was extremely hard for me to bite my tongue. I couldn't stand that bitch and I wasn't about to sit here and act like I felt sorry for her. After she did that shiesty shit with Enzo, she and I could never be in the same room again without me wanting to pop her one. Not that she was really a threat, but Enzo was a man and a man who loved pussy, so I wasn't about to let any bitch steal him away.

After we ate I headed back to my condo, only to find Enzo sitting waiting for me looking as if he'd lost his best friend.

"Hey, wasn't expecting to see you here. What's wrong?" I said, setting my bag on the end table and walking over to the sofa where he was sitting.

"My son's mom is missing," he said, looking down at the floor.

"Your son's mom? I didn't even know you had a son, Enzo," I said, shocked.

"Well, now you know, all right?" he snapped. "She didn't pick him up from school and nobody knows where she is. I can't believe this bitch left him like that," he yelled. He was visibly angry, but clearly the anger was mixed with pain, as if he still had deep feelings for her. I wasn't trying to be insensitive, but I wasn't sure if her missing-person status was so bad after all.

"I'm sorry, Enzo. Is there anything I can do?" I asked, placing my hand on his shoulder.

"I might need you to pick him up from school for the rest of the week until I get shit squared away."

"Okay, that's no problem. Just leave me the information and I'll be there."

"All right. I appreciate it," he said before kissing me on the cheek. "Sorry for snapping. I'm just stressed out." He stood from the chair.

"It's okay. I understand," I replied while standing to walk him to the door.

He wrote down the school information on a Post-it and hugged me before leaving.

"Great, now I'm going to be a damn babysitter," I said aloud. I looked at the clock and noticed that it was almost four, so I would need to leave now to make it to his school by five p.m. I grabbed my bag off of the table and headed back out to the parking lot.

As I made my way across town all sorts of thoughts were flowing through my mind. I'd never been great with children. Honestly, I didn't really like them all that much, which was why I hadn't had any of my own. Now, I had to put on a happy face and play mommy to a little boy that I didn't even know. I didn't even know how old he was but I figured he was preschool age because the name of the school sounded more like a daycare center than an elementary school.

I arrived at the school about fifteen minutes early. I was a ball of nerves as I exited my car and walked over to the building and pressed the bell. Once I was buzzed in I walked over to the receptionist's desk. There were at least fifteen children inside the play area playing with various toys. The level of noise was another reason why I remained childless.

"Hi, can I help you?" the dark-skinned woman said from behind the counter.

"Yes. My name is Sapphire. I was told to ask for a Ms. Jackson."

"Yes, I'm Ms. Jackson. You're here to pick up Elijah."

"Yes, I am."

"Such a shame Tina's gone missing. She's so good with him I can't see her just walking away like that."

"Yes, it is a shame," I replied. Inside I was burning up. I'd heard the name Tina more than I'd like to at this point.

"Well, let me go get him for you," she said, standing from her seated position. A few moments later she returned with the cutest little boy I'd ever seen. He looked just like Enzo but with curly hair and hazel eyes. I smiled, hoping to remove a little bit of the awkwardness since he'd never seen me a day in his life. I could only imagine what he'd been going through with his mother walking out on him.

"Hi, Elijah, I'm Sandra. Your dad sent me to pick you up," I said, kneeling down to his level.

He smiled but remained quiet. I stood up and thanked Ms. Jackson before grabbing him by the hand and leading him out of the building. I didn't have a car seat so I strapped him inside the car the best way I could. He still sat quiet with his teddy bear in hand. Once I got inside the car I looked back at him as he looked up at me.

"Are you okay?" I asked, not really sure what to say to him.

"Yes," he replied.

"How old are you, Elijah?" I asked, feeling more confident since he was talking to me.

"Four," he said, putting up four fingers on his left hand.

"Are you hungry? Do you want some McDonald's?"

"Yes," he said, excited.

"Okay," I said with a giggle. Kids loved McDonald's so I figured that would help him warm up to me.

After going to get him a Happy Meal I headed back to my condo. I hadn't heard from Enzo with any further instruction on what to do with him so I thought the best thing to do was wait for his call. We entered the building and as soon as I was about to open the door the nosy bitch Jessica appeared out of nowhere. If I didn't know any better I'd have sworn her ass was stalking me.

"Is that Mr. Elijah? Hey, honey, long time no see," she said as he ran down the hall toward her to hug her. I quickly followed him.

"I thought you didn't know Tina," she said with a twisted lip.

"I don't know her," I snapped.

"Well, you know her son," she said with her hand on her hip.

"Listen, I don't have to explain shit to you, okay?" I snapped, getting close to her. I was about ready to bust this bitch in the face but I tried to keep my composure because of Elijah. I didn't need Enzo pissed at me for fighting in front of his son, especially since he entrusted me with his most prized possession.

"Umm, there is a child out here so watch your language."

"Hey, Elijah, let me take you in before your food gets cold." I smiled and walked him to the apartment. I quickly closed the door and walked back over to her. "Listen, bitch, I've told you once to stay the fuck away from me and mines. I'm not going to repeat that shit next time."

"I'm not afraid of you. I'm trying to find out what's happened to my friend. I don't give a damn about you or Enzo. She's my friend and I have a right to ask."

"Well, I promise you this: I'll hit your ass with rights and lefts if you don't stay the fuck away from here, all right?" I turned and walked over to my door. I heard her suck her teeth and then walk toward her door. I entered the apartment to find Elijah sitting at the table.

"Is Auntie Jessica coming over?" he asked.

"No, not today, sweetie. I'm waiting on your daddy to call or come pick you up. Besides, she has something to do," I lied.

"Okay."

After he ate I put on the Cartoon Network for him and dialed Enzo. I got his voicemail each time I called. I tried him every fifteen minutes. I began to get irritated the longer I waited for him because I had no clue how to entertain a four-year-old.

After a few hours I decided to give him a bath and dressed him in one of Enzo's T-shirts from my room and the extra underwear he had inside his backpack. Twenty minutes later he was out like a light. Soon I dozed off as well. We were both laid across my king-sized bed.

Enzo crawling into bed behind me awakened me. I felt his arms wrap around me followed by a kiss on my neck.

"Thanks for getting him today, babe. Sorry I missed your calls. I was out trying to figure out where his mom went."

"It's okay. He was really no problem at all. Did you find anything out?" I asked, turning around to face him.

"No, not yet. I'm gonna need you to keep him for a few days. You can take him to school in the morning and pick him up afterward. You'll still have your days free. Just until I figure out what to do."

"Okay," I replied. Though I wasn't excited about it I felt like this was a way to prove to Enzo that I would do anything for him. I was his ride or die and there wasn't any denying that. I was going to suck it up and make the best of the situation. After all, he was a good kid so I didn't see why it would be a problem, and I didn't do shit but shop during the day anyhow.

"I love you," he said, kissing me on the forehead.

"I love you too," I replied. I was smiling from the inside out. This was the part of him that I'd missed and now I had my man back. Tina being gone was just the medicine our injured relationship needed.

Chapter Eleven

Shekia

Lucky Victim

"You really think you can just walk away from me? I don't know who got in your head but I know one mutha-fuckin' thing, you better have your ass on that corner tomorrow morning or you're gonna fuck around and wind up missing," Mannie yelled through the receiver.

He was furious that I hadn't been to work all week. I'd lied and told him that I was sick and had to go in the hospital, but he wasn't buying it. The only reason that I answered the phone to begin with was because I hadn't heard from Enzo in two days. I understood that he needed to deal with the issue of his missing ex; however, he made a promise to me and I could end up hurt because he'd backed out on me once again. Sure you could call me stupid but I believed in him because I wanted to believe that there was actually a way out of this. I lied to my mother as well because I knew if I'd actually left the house he'd find me; therefore, I stayed in my room all day crying from phantom stomach pains and headaches. I kept the door locked to avoid my sister as well. I didn't have time for her annoying-ass lectures.

I waited by the phone for days hoping that Enzo would call but he never did. The next morning, I got up and headed out to meet Mannie. I couldn't fake being sick anymore without my mother taking me to the doctor, revealing the truth, so I had to go. As expected, Mannie was there on time. As soon as I got inside the car he grabbed a handful of my hair and forcefully pulled me over near him.

"If you ever fuck with my money again I promise you I will break your fucking face," he yelled with spit flying in various directions. He popped me in the forehead before letting my hair go and shoving me over toward the window.

A few tears made their way down my cheeks. I quickly grabbed a piece of tissue from my schoolbag and wiped my face, hoping I hadn't messed up my makeup, since that would only piss him off further. I sat quietly as he drove over to the motel. Once we stopped he reached over and grabbed me by the chin to examine my face.

"When you get in there go straight to the bathroom and fix your makeup. The customer will be here in twenty minutes."

"Okay," I replied, grabbing the door handle and exiting the car. I hurried up to the room to do as I was instructed. The last thing I wanted to do was get on his bad side. As promised the customer entered the room twenty minutes later.

"I'll be out in one second," I yelled from the bathroom.

I took out my perfume and sprayed it in all the right places and used my breath freshener before leaving the bathroom. I took a deep breath and smiled as I walked out in my dress, panty-less with four-inch heels.

"Damn, you lookin' good, girl. He didn't tell me he had bitches this fine," the man said, grabbing his crotch. "Turn around for me; let me see what you're working with," he said while licking his thick lips.

For a change the customer wasn't hard on the eye. He actually was pretty fine, just like Enzo. I couldn't understand why men who were this attractive would need to use a prostitute. I did as he asked and slowly spun around to give him a view of my entire body. I did it as sensually as I could in my stiletto heels. When I stopped and was facing him again he'd already taken his dick out of his pants and was stroking it. It was long and extremely thick. I hadn't had one so large and I was almost afraid of it at first sight.

"Come on over here and suck daddy's dick," he grunted. His dick was actually getting longer as he continued to stroke it.

I walked over and got down on my knees in front of him and grabbed hold of the enormous tool. I wrapped my lips around it and in one swift motion took the whole thing inside of my mouth. My jaws were tired within a few minutes of tackling his monster. He moaned and groaned the entire time as he periodically lifted his hips off of the bed to force it deeper into my throat. I was hoping that I was doing a good job. Such a good job that he'd cum fast and end this session. I continued working on him for over fifteen minutes before he stopped me. He grabbed a condom from the bedside table and opened it.

"Get on your knees on the edge of the bed. I want to get in that ass of yours."

I was slightly trembling at the thought of that huge dick going inside of my tiny asshole. I couldn't tell him no or show that I was afraid because an unsatisfied customer would land me a beating at the end of the day. So I assumed the doggie-style position, arched my back, and pointed my ass up in the air as far as I could. I could hear him spitting into his hand and wetting his protected shaft before he used both of his hands to spread my ass cheeks apart. I sucked in some air as I braced myself for the pain that I was sure I was about to endure. Without hesitation he shoved his entire dick inside of my tight asshole, immediately causing my knees to buckle. I fell down on the bed and his dick slipped out.

"Don't run, girl, I'm gonna give it to you real good," he said.

He grabbed me around my waist and pulled me back up. This time when he entered me he held on to me so I couldn't move. I could feel the skin around my asshole ripping as he stuffed his dick inside of me. I wanted to scream but I bit my lip and held it in.

"Stop tensing up it won't hurt so much," he said as he continued to move in and out of me.

I wasn't sure how you could relax with your insides feeling like they're being torn apart but I tried my best. I stayed positioned and locked my elbows to support myself. A single tear dropped from my eye onto the bed but I held back any more evidence of my pain. He pounded me for at least another half hour until he finally came and removed himself from my swollen tunnel.

"That was great. You'll definitely be seeing me again wit' your sexy ass," he said as he pulled the condom off and tossed it into the trashcan beside the bed.

He headed into the bathroom and a few minutes later emerged. I was sitting on the edge of the bed waiting for him to leave so I could clean myself up.

"Thanks again," he said, walking to the door and leaving out of the room.

I got up and wobbled to the bathroom. My ass was on fire. I locked the door behind me and turned the water on. A few seconds later Mannie was outside of the door banging on it.

"Hurry up in there. I got more work for you," he yelled.

"Okay," I responded.

I dreaded having to see another customer. I was in so much pain I could barely walk. I grabbed a washcloth and soap to clean up, and, just as I thought, it was covered with blood from the damage. I rinsed out the washcloth and covered it with soap again.

Just as I was about to set the soap down I heard Mannie in a heated conversation with someone. I hurried and finished up and straightened up my clothing. I was about to open the door when I heard a loud boom. It sounded like a gunshot. Immediately I dropped down to the floor, afraid for my life. A second later there was banging on the bathroom door.

"Shekia, open the door. It's Enzo."

I jumped up from the floor and opened the door. He grabbed me by the hand and pulled me out of the bathroom.

"We gotta go now; the cops will be here soon."

I looked over at Mannie's lifeless body lying on the floor with blood beginning to seep into the carpet. I didn't ask any questions. I ran out of the room with Enzo and down the stairs to a waiting car. There was a guy sitting behind the wheel waiting for us. We jumped into the back seat and he sped out of the parking lot and onto the street. I was still quiet. I didn't know what had just happened and I wasn't sure if I wanted to know. The less I knew was probably better.

We drove through the city until we pulled up in front of a parking garage where he drove inside and went down to the lower level and parked. They got out of the car and Enzo pulled me out as well. He and the driver gave each other a quick handshake before he walked over to a parked BMW and got inside. Enzo's car was also parked on the same level. We got inside of his car before he said anything to me.

"Are you okay?" he asked while starting the car.

"What happened back there?" I asked.

"Doesn't matter. I asked you were you okay?" he responded.

"Yes, Enzo, I'm okay."

"Good. I'm taking you home. You won't have to worry about that nigga anymore. I need you to call me in the morning and I'll come get you so we can talk."

"Will you answer me this time?"

"Shekia, I got a lot of shit going on in my life right now but I'm a man of my word. I told you that I would be there for you and I have been. Shit is just a little hectic on my side. I just need you to do what I'm asking you to do right now and I promise things will be good from here on out."

"All right," I replied.

The rest of the ride we were both silent. I was afraid to say anything else but I was glad that he'd taken care of Mannie. I no longer had to look over my shoulder and wonder if he'd be watching me. I no longer would be forced to prostitute my body for a living. I was overwhelmed with emotions but I held it all together. Once he dropped me off, I saw that my mother's car wasn't outside, which was good. I could slip into my room undetected.

"Call me at eight," he said.

I nodded and got out of the car. He drove off as soon as I opened the door to my house. I hurried upstairs and went into my room. I locked the door, turned on my radio, and flopped down on the bed, burying my face into the pillow. I began to sob uncontrollably. So much had happened in my life and for the life of me I couldn't figure out why. What had I done to deserve all of it? I wondered what it was that God was trying to tell me. I was all ears; I needed to see it so that I could make some changes in my life. After crying for over an hour or so I finally dozed off.

Chapter Twelve

Milan

Reason to Fall in Love Again

I hadn't seen Shekia since our argument, which was probably a good thing because we both probably needed some time to breathe. I wasn't trying to fight with her. I actually wanted our relationship to grow stronger but we were both very different people now. Spending so much time apart we went in two totally different directions in our lives. The fact that she was my sister was enough for me to want to go hard for her. I wanted her to live a better life and possibly turn out even better than me. The week was flying by and I was honestly extremely exhausted. I had retreated to my room to relax when the phone rang.

"Hey, Milan, I was calling to see if you were ready," Mike said.

Shit, I had completely forgotten about our date.

"Yeah, do you need my address?" I said, acting as if I was expecting him. I wasn't really in the mood to go out and I wasn't really optimistic about feeling any different. I wasn't in the best of moods but I thought maybe going with him could be just the medicine I needed to clear my mind.

"Yeah."

I gave him the address and as soon as I hung up I ran through the house like I was in a race trying to find something to wear. I quickly jumped in the shower and as I was fixing my hair the doorbell rang. *Damn,* I thought. *That was record time.*

Once he arrived I became excited about the date. From what I remembered, Mike was a good-looking brother and I could certainly use some companionship. Though I had my eyes on Devon, I had learned from past experience to never get my hopes up too high too soon. I also learned to never let myself get played again. There would be no replay of Amir for me.

"Wow, you look good," he said as I opened the door.

"Thanks," I replied.

"So, where are we headed?" I asked, anticipating enjoying myself. I prayed that this date would turn out as I expected.

"It's a surprise. Do you like surprises?" he asked, reaching his hand out for me to grab hold of it.

"I love surprises!" I admitted before grabbing his hand and closing the door behind me.

We drove for what seemed like an eternity before arriving at a restaurant in New Jersey called Mélange. It was a black-owned Southern and Italian cuisine restaurant. I fell in love with it immediately. It was small and quiet. The dim lighting and candles on the tables made the mood very romantic. We were seated at the table that he had reserved. It was a bring-your-own-bottle restaurant so he impressed me by bringing a bottle of Dom Pérignon.

"This is a really nice restaurant, Mike. I'm impressed," I said honestly.

"Why, I don't look like a classy dude?" he asked with a smile.

"Oh, no," I said, embarrassed. "You look very classy. I just didn't expect you to bring me here on a first date. I'm sure it's really expensive, since the menus don't have prices on them." I laughed.

Joining in the laughter, he replied, "Damn, you noticed that? That's funny, but the money isn't an object for me. You're a beautiful lady and I don't mind treating you well. Stick around and you'll see I have a lot to offer," he said.

Damn, he looked even better being suave. Though his words could have been genuine, it was hard for me to believe what men said. He was turning me on though, and if things went well, I would keep him around. Even if it was just to be a friend, he was good company.

"Well, I appreciate that, Mike. I can certainly get used to a man with good taste," I said, smiling.

The food took an extremely long time to come but they brought out a sample of an appetizer, with red peppers, cheese, oils, and crackers while you waited. I was at first turned off by the look of it and afraid to eat it. It wasn't until the chef came out from the back to greet everyone that I gathered up the heart to try it. How could I not try it with the chef standing there telling me how great it was? Surprisingly it was really good and I was actually glad that I had tried it.

Dinner went off without a hitch and soon we were heading out of the restaurant. I wondered what he had planned next. I was a little tipsy but could stand for a little more fun.

"So, where are we headed to now?" I asked as I opened the passenger side door.

"I was going to take you home, but if you can think of somewhere else you'd like to go I'm all for it," he replied.

"Why don't we go out to Penn's Landing and walk around, enjoy the night air," I suggested.

"At this time of night? Are you crazy?" He laughed.

"Yeah, maybe that's not such a good idea. I can't think of anything else to do. I just know that I'm not ready for this night to be over," I said as we both sat down in our seats.

"We can always go to my spot if you'd like to," he said.

I gave him a quick stare and replied, "Your spot, huh?"

"I'm just saying, I can't think of anywhere else to go either," he quickly defended his intentions.

"That's cool. We can go to your place."

"Okay, then we are on our way," he replied before turning the car on and starting the drive.

Soon we were pulling up in front of his South Philly apartment. I was nervous about going in for some reason. I didn't want him to get the wrong idea about me. It's not like I planned on having sex with him, but he was fine, I was tipsy, and it had been a while since the last time I had sex, so who knew what could happen?

While heading up the stairs to his second-floor apartment, I slowly followed him. After going inside, I was shocked at how neat everything was. The place looked like no one lived there.

"Damn, it's so neat in here. Is this really your place?" I joked.

"Yeah, it's my place. I'm just a neat freak. Can't stand clutter and dirt."

"That's cool," I said as I took a look around. His color scheme was natural browns and greens that blended nicely. He had brown leather furniture with cream stone tables and glass tops. He had a large TV with a huge surround-sound system. I could get used to spending time there. Everything about it felt so comfortable. I took a seat on the sofa and instantly took off my shoes.

"I see you don't waste time getting comfortable." He laughed.

"No, I don't," I agreed.

He came over and sat next to me. I could feel the heat from his body. I wanted to get up and leave because the temptation was killing me. He turned to look at me and I quickly turned away, embarrassed that I had been staring.

"What's wrong? What are you thinking about?" he asked.

"Nothing," I lied.

"Really, what are you thinking about?"

"I like you, Mike, and I didn't expect to."

"Damn, well, at least you're honest."

"No, really, I had a crazy ending to my last relationship and I'm still kind of bitter. I thought that I wouldn't let myself love or even like another person after being hurt and it's still fresh. But you're a nice guy and I couldn't take what someone else did out on you. I think that we can be really good friends, and who knows what will happen?" I said, moving closer to him.

"Well, I'm glad that you didn't and I'm glad that you like me because I really like you," he said as he stared me in the eyes.

I decided to just go with my heart and kiss him. I couldn't resist as he licked his sexy-ass lips after each sentence. I knew that he wouldn't turn me away and at that moment I felt like being daring. I moved in and softly touched his lips with mine. He returned the kiss and slowly placed his hand on my thigh. I thought, *Damn, he isn't wasting any time,* but neither was I. I guessed we both felt the same way. He moved his kisses from my lips to my neck as I tilted my head to the side to give him enough space. My panties were getting wet as he caressed my thighs and French kissed my neck. The movements of his tongue were slow but steady as I tried to control myself.

"Stand up and undress," he ordered. I got up from the sofa and obeyed. As he watched me he began to undress as well. I was glad to see that he was blessed down below when I saw his hard soldier standing at attention. My mouth was watering and had this meeting been after we'd known each other longer I would have gotten down on my knees and put my tongue to work. I didn't want him to think that I just get down for anyone so I held in the urge and instead let him take control.

"Turn around. I want to admire every inch of you." He continued to make demands and they were all turning me on.

I couldn't let him know how excited I really was but it was so hard not to. Every time I got a glimpse of his muscular, sexy chocolate ass I wanted to jump on him. Instead I kept my cool and went along with it.

"Do you like what you see?" I had made a full circle and was now staring at him as he stood opposite of me holding his hard dick in his hand. He smiled when he noticed the look I gave him when I noticed.

"What's that look for? I didn't scare you, did I?"

"No, if it's one thing about me that's a fact, it's that I ain't never scared." I let out a girlish giggle.

"Well, come over here and get it then."

I didn't waste any time. I was damn near running to make my way over to him. I was in desperate need of some sexual healing for sure. I stared him in the eye and met his lips with mine. His hands were around my waist tickling the small of my back. His lips were softer than mine, and him rubbing against me made me more excited than I'd been about sex in a long time. I could just imagine those lips touching my pussy. I was sure to melt all over them.

We both were breathing heavily when he picked me up off the ground and tightly gripped my waist. I wrapped my long legs around him and with ease he slid his dick inside of my pussy. I almost burst on contact. All of my adrenaline rushed to that spot, and as a moan escaped his mouth my walls began to contract gripping him like I was milking a cow. He held on to my ass and lifted it up each time I pushed down, fitting every inch of him inside of my juicy tunnel. Together we created a flawless rhythm and this episode of mind-blowing intimacy was one that I wouldn't soon forget.

He took steps back toward the sofa but still held me in the same position. I loved a strong man and the fact that he'd had me in the air for the past fifteen minutes was proof of that. I was soon lying down on the sofa with him on top of me and we hadn't been separated for even a second while making the transition.

"Is it good to you, baby? I need to hear you speak."

I was enjoying myself too much to let out a word. I feared that I would lose my concentration and not be able to cum. I lay there silent with my eyes closed until he stopped mid-stroke.

"What's wrong?" I asked.

"I mean if you're not enjoying it there's no reason to keep going," he replied with a devilish grin.

"Of course I'm enjoying it. Don't you hear all the noise I'm making?"

"That could just be an act."

"I'm not acting, okay? Now keep giving it to me so I can show you exactly how much I'm enjoying it."

He smiled and a few seconds later he was pounding me again. I was screaming, moaning, and yelling his name among other things. I couldn't walk away from this without cumming so I had to perform as he wanted me to. We were both dripping with sweat and breathing heavily when I felt his body heating up. I palmed his ass to pull him in closer to me and instantly my body began to shake and my juices were leaking out all over the sofa. He followed right behind me trembling. He quickly pulled out of me, grabbed hold of his dick and released onto my stomach. I can admit that I was a little grossed out by that but not enough to change my mood. Hell, it was better that he put it there than letting it out inside of me.

"Man that was good." He wiped his forehead and sat down at the opposite end of the sofa. I was still lying flat on my back with one of my legs behind his back and the other across his lap.

"Yes, it was." I laughed. "Where's your bathroom?"

"Straight up the steps to your left; washcloths are in the cabinet."

I peeled myself from the couch and walked toward the stairs. He smacked me on my ass as I walked away. I turned around and gave him a giggle. Once I entered the bathroom and locked the door behind me I grabbed a washcloth from the cabinet behind the door and turned on the sink. Of course my instincts told me to look around. I mean, who wouldn't try to find out more about someone you just met and screwed? Inside the medicine cabinet were different items including acne cream, cold medication, and shaving cream, but one thing stood out to me the most: a prescription bottle with a female's name on it.

So he has a woman? I thought. I mean it's not like I had asked him but why would he bring me into his home? As I thought about it more items stood out. There was a makeup kit on top of the counter, and a pink bottle of lotion under the sink. I wasn't angry but I was a little annoyed. I decided not to let it show. I didn't want to ruin the evening that we'd just had so I cleaned up and quietly headed back downstairs to get dressed.

"You want to stay the night or you want me to drive you home?"

"You can drive me home. I have to get up pretty early in the morning," I lied. I didn't want someone to walk in on us, starting an altercation.

"Cool, let me go wipe off and I'll take you."

I grabbed my clothes from the floor and put them on piece by piece. I was dressed and ready to go in record time.

Soon we were on the expressway and sitting quietly. Before leaving, we hugged and I promised that I would call him the next day. I didn't believe that I would, it just seemed like the perfect thing to say at the time. It was also the way I had to end the night to avoid talking about the fact that I knew he belonged to someone else. To me, it not only meant that he was a cheater, but I wouldn't be able to have him to myself. Because of his relationship status, there wasn't really any reason to move forward with our friendship.

Chapter Thirteen

Sapphire

WTF?

"I'll be back to pick you up later, okay? Be a good boy," I said as I waved good-bye to Elijah.

There hadn't been any more new developments since Enzo asked me to watch Elijah. Tina was still missing and Enzo was still on a mission to find her. I hadn't seen much of him besides the evenings when he'd come and climb into bed. I wasn't sure what was going on with him mentally but I was sure hoping that she wouldn't be found. I believed he'd eventually get used to her absence and grow closer to me because I'd had his back.

After dropping Elijah off I decided to go to the hair salon. I'd missed my last appointment and I needed to look my best at all times. I drove down to the salon on Woodland Avenue and parked. As I turned the car off and was about to open the door Enzo's car drove right by me and inside was a female passenger I didn't recognize. I immediately restarted the car and made a U-turn in the middle of street. The driver of the car I'd cut off was yelling and cursing behind the wheel. I flipped him the bird and continued on my mission. I'd be damned if I was going to continue playing babysitter while he spent his free time with another bitch. I wasn't even going out like that.

I sped up and kept on the tail of the Honda Accord that was in between his car and mine. We stopped at a light and I got nervous. I was hoping that he wouldn't see me but if he did I was surely going to give him a piece of my mind.

I followed him through the city and after making a couple quick stops he drove to an apartment building that I wasn't familiar with. The combination of his store runs consisted of a Jamaican food restaurant, a Wine & Spirits, and a CVS. Those three stores told me he was planning on doing more than I'd like to imagine with his female passenger.

Once he parked he walked around to the passenger side and politely opened the door for the female. My jaw dropped at the sight of him acting like a gentleman. When she stepped out I noticed how young she looked. She wasn't dressed special and was actually wearing a school bag on her back. Now I was even more curious about her identity. I watched them go into the building and there wasn't much more I could do at that point because I didn't have a clue which apartment they'd entered. Feeling defeated I drove off. I was beyond pissed but I knew confronting him would only end up in a shouting match. I had no hard proof that he was sleeping with her, and since I didn't know all of his family I'd feel like a fool if she'd turned out to be a relative.

The following day was pretty much the same until he informed me that Elijah's grandmother was going to be keeping him from that point on. Though I was relieved I didn't let him know that. I actually played it off as if I was sad to see him go. With my days free I made it my point to find out who the hell the young female was I'd seen him with. I was going to put on my private investigator hat and see what was really going on.

I trailed him for most of the day but I didn't see anything unusual. The female I'd seen the previous day was nowhere to be found. I was relieved. I continued with the rest of my day as planned. Once I made it back to the apartment I was shocked by the huge spectacle going on outside. There was police tape around the perimeter and news vans were everywhere. I didn't know many people in the building besides a young couple I'd speak to in passing and the pain in the ass down the hall. I walked over to the couple, Mark and Lisa, who were standing amid the crowd of onlookers.

"Hey, Lisa, what's going on?" I asked.

"They found that girl Jessica dead in her apartment," she replied.

"Really? Oh, my that's scary. Did they say what happened to her?"

"No, not yet. They aren't letting anyone in, but the person who found her said that her apartment looked like there had been a struggle, like a fight. You live right down the hall. You didn't hear anything?" Mark asked.

"No, I didn't hear anything at all. That makes you want to add extra locks to your door, doesn't it?" I asked.

"It sure does," Lisa agreed.

"That's why I keep my gun loaded and right near the bed. I'll kill a muthafucker if they come in my damn apartment."

"I know that's right!" I said. "Well, I'm not going to just stand out here all night and wait. I'm gonna go. I will see you all later."

I'd be damned if I was going to stand for hours in six-inch heels. I could find better shit to do with my time. I wasn't really sure where I was going to go. I hated my family and I didn't know where the hell Enzo was. The only place I figured that I could go and chill was the Velvet Rope. I would've preferred to spend my free time with my man but he was missing in action and I wasn't about to sit around like a lost puppy waiting for him.

I headed over to the club and was greeted by a bouncer named Brill. He was actually the bouncer who pulled me away from beating Eliza half to death.

"What's up, champ? Long time no see." He smiled.

"What's been up?"

"Same ol'. You heard what happened to E?"

"Yeah, I heard. Did they find out who did it yet?"

"Naw, but people talking. You know how that shit go. Anyway what's up with you? Are you still single? I know that nigga you was fighting over stayed up in here throwing E bills. I knew you'd be done with him sooner or later."

"No, we're actually still together," I responded, a bit annoyed.

"Oh, shit, my bad. I didn't know. Let me zip my lips." He laughed. "Jannie in there; I'm assuming that's who you came to see."

"Yeah, I did. Well, it was good seeing you."

"Good seeing you too," he said before opening the door to let me in.

I entered the club and waved to the girl sitting at the door. I smiled when I saw Jannie dancing behind the bar. I'd missed coming in and seeing her face. She was always the face that convinced me to come back regardless of how many times I wanted to turn around and walk the other way. Working in this environment you're degraded in more ways than you would ever imagine are possible.

"Hey, girl! What are you doing here?" she yelled.

I hugged her over the bar before taking a seat on a stool. "Girl, my damn apartment building is a crime scene. Shit was all taped up." I shook my head.

"Really? What the hell happened?" she asked while pouring me a drink.

"Some girl was murdered. She probably deserved it. Bitch was always in somebody's business."

"Damn, Sapphire, that's cold."

"That's real shit. You can't keep fucking with people and think you're going to remain untouched."

"Yeah, you're right about that."

"So let me ask you something. Have you seen Enzo in here?"

"Naw, not since Eliza got attacked."

"How come you never told me about him and her? I mean you're supposed to be my girl and you never once told me he was in here throwing money at her."

"You know I stay out of people's business, Sapphire. Besides, I knew you'd find out eventually."

"So you just don't tell me?"

"No, because I don't get in the middle of other people's relationships. I stay in my own lane and worry about my own shit. I'm sorry, girl, but that's just the way I roll."

"Well, let's just be glad she isn't here anymore to fuck with my man," I replied.

Jannie stared at me for a moment. I knew my response was raw but it was the way I felt. I didn't give a shit about anyone who had the balls to impede on my relationship.

After finishing our conversation and finishing off my drink, I headed home. The atmosphere in the club just wasn't the place I wanted to be. Though without Enzo I probably would've still been working there my new life was much better than my old one. It was a memory that I didn't mind leaving behind. There was a time that I didn't think I could do anything else but I knew now that I could do much better.

By the time I arrived we were allowed back into the building. The crime scene investigators were still on the floor once I made it to my door. I stuck my key in before a woman's voice called out to me.

"Excuse me, miss. Can I speak with you for a moment?"

I stopped and turned around. "How can I help you?" I asked with one hand on my handle.

"I wanted to ask you a few questions about last evening. Did you hear anything out of the norm?"

"No, actually. I wasn't here, sorry," I lied. I wasn't really in the mood to be involved.

"Were you friends with the victim?"

"No, I wasn't. Look I have to work in the morning. I really wish I could help but I can't," I lied.

"Okay. Well, here is my card. If you think of anything please give us a call," she said, passing me a business card.

"Okay." I took the card and closed the door.

Chapter Fourteen

Shekia

Life Altered

"You really thought you could just steal my man, huh?" The erratic woman paced the floor. I didn't know who she was or what she was even talking about.

"I really don't know what you are talking about. Please let me go," I pleaded.

She was waving a gun around and mumbling under her breath. "Soon as he gets here we are going to settle this. I've worked too hard for my relationship," she yelled.

"Who are you talking about? Who is your man?"

"Who is my man? The nigga you've been with almost every day. Stop acting, stupid bitch, you know exactly who I'm talking about."

"I'm not having sex with Enzo. He's just my friend. He was just helping me out."

"I guess I'm Boo Boo the fool, huh?" she yelled.

"It's the truth." I tried to be as calm as possible, though inside I was falling apart. She had both of my hands tied to the back of the chair that I was sitting in. My head was throbbing from the bump that she'd created when she hit me from behind. I didn't know what else to say because she clearly had her mind set on making me pay for a pseudo relationship. I prayed that Enzo would get there soon to save me as he'd always done. He was always on time.

"What the fuck are you doing, Sapphire?" Enzo yelled as he entered the apartment and slammed the door.

"I'm taking care of your little side bitch here. Same as I did with all the others," she yelled.

"What the hell are you talking about? I'm not sleeping with her and what others?"

"The others: Tina, Eliza, Lisa. I took care of them. I got them out of our lives so it could just be you and me."

"What?" he yelled. He began to walk over to her until she raised the gun.

"Don't do it. Unless you want a hole in your chest." she screamed. "Everything that I've done for you. I've had your back over and over again and all you did was give me your ass to kiss. You know I'm not a fool. You made me believe that I was the only woman you wanted. It didn't take the nosy bitch down the hall to throw Tina in my face! I followed you. You told me your last relationship was through but all you did was move her to a huge house and move me into the condo. Then to add insult to injury you start fucking with this bitch!"

"Sandra, you really need to let her go. She's just a kid. I'm not fucking her," he yelled. "Put the damn gun down before you hurt someone."

"I'm not going to do that. If I have to kill you and myself so you can stop fucking other people I will," she yelled.

I sat silently because I didn't want to say anything to piss her off further. I was hoping that he could talk her down but the more she spoke the more irrational her sentences were.

"Listen to yourself. You really want to kill yourself? Really, Sandra? None of those women deserved to be hurt like that."

"And I did? I deserved to be hurt?"

"I didn't say that but you just told me that you are the reason my son doesn't have his mother. You really think I could be with you after this?"

"You don't have a choice! You will be with me even if it's in death."

I sat there still quiet as I slowly wiggled my hands free from the shoestrings she'd used to restrain me. I was hoping that she'd be distracted enough for me to eventually make a run for it.

"Put the fucking gun down!" he yelled again.

She kept her hand steady. He was slowly reaching into the back of his pants to retrieve his gun.

"What are you doing?" she asked. "Put your hands down!" she screamed at him.

In one swift motion Enzo pulled his gun from his waist. I jumped out of the chair and hit the floor. I heard four concurrent shots fired and two loud thuds followed by silence. I slowly got up from the floor and there lay both of them, shot and bloodied. I ran over to Enzo, who was at that point coughing up blood. His body was shivering. I didn't know what to do. I ran to the phone and called 911 before tending to his wounds. I didn't care about her. She'd hurt the only real friend I'd ever had.

"Hold on, Enzo, okay? The ambulance is coming." Tears were beginning to form in my eyes. It was all my fault. Because he'd tried to help me he'd been hurt. "Enzo. Enzo . . . Enzo," I screamed. His eyes were now closed and his body had stopped moving. I began to shake him. "Wake up, Enzo, please wake up. You can't die on me."

I sat there as his body was drained of life. He was gone and there wasn't anything that I could do about it. I was still sobbing when the paramedics and police arrived. I couldn't speak. I was in a state of shock. I thought about the time I'd spent with him and how much he'd done.

I was taken from the scene to the police station and sat there for hours as they took my statement. My heart was heavy but I felt relieved when they informed me that she'd died as well. She didn't deserve to live after all she'd done. I told them everything. I even gave them the short list of names that she'd spat during their confrontation.

After they were done questioning me I was taken home. I didn't want to talk to my mother or sister about what'd gone on. I wasn't in the mood for a speech or any "I told you so's." I retreated to my bedroom and buried my head in my pillow to cry. A few minutes later there was a knock on my bedroom door.

"Shekia, the phone is for you," my mother said from the opposite side of the door.

"Okay," I replied.

I didn't feel like talking. I'd had the worst day of my life and I couldn't imagine who'd be calling. I got up off the bed and walked over to the phone to pick it up.

"Hello," I said.

"I'm back, bitch. Thought your little boyfriend got me? Well, think again. I don't die that easily. Now be outside at the normal time tomorrow," Mannie yelled. Chills went up and down my spine at that moment.

Click.

I thought my life couldn't get any worse. Mannie was still alive and with Enzo gone I had no other choice but to return or I'd suffer for it. I slowly put the phone down and slid down to the floor. I got on my knees and questioned God. I didn't understand what I was being punished for.

I fell asleep on the floor in that very spot after hours of crying. At that point, I knew my life would be ending pretty soon and, honestly, I'd probably be better off dead anyhow.

Chapter Fifteen

Milan

Appreciate Me

I woke up the next morning with absolutely nothing to do. The phone began ringing as I was watching my morning talk shows. I looked at the caller ID and noticed that it was Danell. After letting it ring a fourth time I answered it.

"Hello."

"What's up, girl, why haven't you called me?" she asked, clearly unaware of the fact that I had a newfound grudge.

"I had a lot of things on my mind and I didn't feel like being bothered," I said honestly.

"Well, are you going to the club tonight?" she asked, totally missing my sarcasm.

"No, I really don't feel like it."

"What's wrong with you?"

"Nothing, I just don't feel like it," I responded loudly.

"All right, well, I'll talk to you later since you're in such a shitty mood," she replied.

Click.

I hung up without a response. I immediately began to block her out of my mind. I couldn't hang around her and keep a straight face since I was still annoyed with the love triangle. There was no way that I could fake my feelings and at this point she was the chick who'd stolen my man. The fact that she didn't know he was my man didn't matter to me. Honestly, our friendship was the only thing keeping me from busting her in the face, but had this been a few years prior that wouldn't have stopped me either. I knew that I was being petty by not hanging around her but so what! I couldn't have that close relationship with her knowing that we were having sex with the same man. I also couldn't get over the fact that he would cheat on me with her. You would think he could find someone better than me. She wasn't even close to my level.

I searched through my bags for something to wear to my upcoming date with Devon and I didn't have any luck. I figured that a mall run might be in order. I couldn't go out looking like anything less than the best. After the phone call with Danell, I needed to vent. If there was one person in the world who would understand the way that I felt about the situation it was Tramaine. She picked up on the second ring.

"Hey, what's up?" she asked.

"Girl, you know Danell called me today?"

"For what? After that shit that happened I wouldn't have even answered the phone."

"She wanted to know why I haven't called her. I simply told her that I was busy."

"You should have told her the truth. She thinks she's all that. It would burst her little bubble if she found out that Amir was yours first."

"I don't really even care anymore. I just had to tell someone about it. Maybe with the cold shoulder she'll get the point that I don't want to be bothered." I laughed. "But enough about her; guess what I'm doing tonight."

"What?" she asked, excited.

"I'm going out with Devon!" I said as I smiled from ear to ear.

"For real? You lucky bitch. You just got back and you're already on date number two. That's what's up, girl! I'm so happy for you." She laughed.

"I know. I just don't know what to wear."

"Put on something sexy, girl, to make his mouth water. Shit I'd be ass naked under a trench coat if I was going out with his fine ass." She burst into laughter.

"Oh, trust me, girl, more than his mouth will be watering by the time I get done with him. I was thinking about going to Saks to pick up this Louis Vuitton bag I wanted to match my shoes."

"Well, if you're going let me know," she said.

"If you're dressed, I can come scoop you because I want to go now."

"Okay, well, come get me."

"Okay, I'm on my way," I said before hanging up.

We headed to Saks on City Avenue and chatted along the way. It was nice to have her around. While I was in Atlanta I rarely hung out with females since most of them were jealous of me and I didn't have time for that shit.

I hit the store with a vengeance, picking up the bag that I wanted and a couple of other things. I knew that I had spent too much money. Tramaine spent almost as much as I did. Some would say that I was out of control when it came to spending money but shit, I had to look good and I worked damn hard for my money. You wouldn't catch me dead and looking a mess. I planned on being shit sharp in my casket.

After we left the mall we went to her house because she wanted me to meet Tyron. She'd been with him for the past few years and was so in love. Deep down, I envied that because I missed having a man around when I wanted one.

Tyron was nice looking, not quite what I imagined, but he appeared to have money. And if I knew anything about Tramaine, any man she was with was paid. I was sure looks were important to her as well but money was definitely at the top of the list. He didn't really have that much conversation either but that was cool because I had things to do. I told her that I would catch up with her later and left.

The day went pretty fast since I didn't do much else. Shekia hadn't shown her face all day. So I had given up on talking to her. She didn't listen anyway so talking was a waste of both breath and time. It was like talking to a brick wall. At this age there wasn't really anything that I could do to help her. I had missed out on so much of her life that she didn't really look up to me the way that she would have had I been here. The more that I tried to get close the more that she seemed to back away. Maybe I needed to get used to the fact that we'd never be close again.

Devon called around five and told me to be ready by eight. I was dressed to kill when he arrived and rang the doorbell. I looked myself over in the mirror one last time to make sure that everything was perfect before I opened the door. I pulled the door open with a smile.

"I see that you're looking lovely as usual," he said, glancing at my figure-hugging dress. I knew at that moment that I was getting the effect that I'd set out for. His mouth was watering and if he could have eaten me right there I was positive that he would have.

"Thanks; you don't look too bad yourself," I said, returning the compliment.

"Well, thanks. So, are you ready for the night of your life?" he asked, extending his hand.

"I sure am. Let me get my jacket."

First he took me to a seafood restaurant in Center City to eat. I wasn't really into all of the fancy seafood but I didn't want to hurt his feelings so I picked something simple from the menu. We talked and caught up on some things. He told me how he'd ended up cutting hair and surprisingly it was always something that he wanted to do. I always pictured him playing some sort of professional sport like basketball or boxing. Back when we were young he was great at everything physical. A barber had never crossed my mind. I was smiling from ear to ear thinking of the possibilities of a relationship with him. I mean, we could be perfect together. With both of our skills and beauty, no one would be able to stop us.

After we ate we headed to the movies and then took a walk down Penn's Landing. I laughed as we walked along, as I thought about Mike. I had suggested this to him and he thought I was crazy. I guessed that he was afraid that someone would rob us or something. Devon looked at me strange when I giggled. I told him that it was nothing and he quickly brushed it off.

"So, how did everything go with your sister?"

"It didn't go anywhere far. She didn't want to hear anything that I had to say. So, I'm done. I'm not going to keep trying for her to push me away," I said.

"Well, she's young and she'll learn. Obviously it'll be the hard way."

"She thinks that she's grown though, that's the problem," I said as I thought about her recent actions.

"It will be all right, she'll learn. I guarantee that," he said, trying to comfort me with hopes that everything would be okay. I didn't believe that. I knew that she was stubborn and I was the same way once. Fortunately I decided to listen and got myself together.

"I hope so," I spoke softly.

"You know when you first left, I thought about you all the time," he said.

"Really?" I asked, shocked that he even admitted that to me. The truth was that I thought about him too. I was just too afraid to let him know it.

"You know how close we were. When I saw you walking down the street, I knew that I should have gotten with you back in the day."

"Well, I was with Tylee then and we were such good friends. I don't think we would have been mature enough to stay friends if things hadn't worked out."

"I always wondered why you really left. Was it him?"

"Somewhat," I replied.

"What do you mean by that?" he asked, confused by the statement.

"I was pregnant," I said, dreading his response. That was a secret that I wanted to carry to the grave but I felt so close to Devon that I knew I had to tell him.

"What? Why didn't you tell me?" he asked, shocked.

"Because I got an abortion and there wasn't anything to tell," I responded.

"Damn, I would have never thought of that. So, is that why you broke up with him?"

"He didn't want anything to do with me once he found out that I was pregnant."

"I bet if he saw you now, he'd be all over you."

"Well, he couldn't have me because now I want you," I blurted out. Damn, I couldn't believe that I had just let the cat out of the bag. I was sure he knew that I was attracted to him but I didn't want him to think I was on him like that.

"So do you think we could be a couple? I mean, do you really think that we can make it work?" he asked, with seriousness in his face.

"I believe that we could make it work," I said, with a huge smile on my face.

"I'm glad to hear that," he said before reaching out to hug me.

His body felt warm, and at this moment I was so glad to be back home. We walked around for a little while longer before he drove me home. I was kind of sad that the night had to end but I knew that I would get to see a lot more of him soon. That was enough to rock me to sleep, nearing a great dream.

The next morning I woke up to a ringing phone. Damn! I hated that. It always happened when I was in a deep sleep, "slobbering on the pillow" type sleep, that someone called to wake me up. I was groggy when I turned over to answer.

"Hello, Ms. Brooks?"

"Yes, this is me," I replied, still annoyed.

"Good morning, my name is Susan and I'm calling from Korman Suites. You put in an application for an apartment. Correct?"

"Yes, I did."

"I'm just calling to let you know that your application was approved. If you can come down this afternoon and fill out the necessary paperwork with your deposit, you can immediately get your keys."

"Really? Wow. I'm so glad to hear that. I can come down about one, is that okay?" I asked, quickly jumping out of my groggy mood.

"Sure, that's fine. I'll mark you in the book."

"Thanks a lot, Susan. I'll see you at one," I replied.

"Sure thing," she said before hanging up.

I was so excited that I was going to get my own place. I would have to run to the bank to get a certified check. I didn't really like writing personal checks because people usually take too long to cash them. I'd rather the money come out immediately.

It was now Friday and I didn't need to report to work until Monday. I wasn't really in a rush to get back to work because I was enjoying the time off. I would be meeting and working with new people. I just prayed that things would start off good. I wasn't real good with making new friends. Women always hated me for my looks since of course none of them looked as good as me. I took pride in the way that I looked and I wasn't going to change that to get people to like me. If I had to go without friends forever it wouldn't make any difference.

I quickly got out of the bed and jumped in the shower. I wanted to get to the bank early before it got packed. Once I was dressed I ate a quick breakfast and headed to the car. As soon as I was about to get in, I heard someone calling my name.

"So, it is true," Tylee spoke loudly.

"What?" I replied sharply.

"That you're back in town. I didn't believe it. I must say, you look damn good," he said, with a devilish grin.

"Thanks," I replied, not really amused by the comment.

"So, I hear you're getting money now."

"Something like that," I replied blandly because I really wanted to end the conversation.

"Well, I wanted to let you know that I missed you."

"I doubt that!" I said, becoming annoyed.

"I did; why you don't believe me? It's been five years. You were the love of my life back in the day."

"It really doesn't matter at this point. You didn't care too much about me when I was knocked up."

"I know that we left off on a bad note but I wanted to see if we could try again."

"I don't believe that you even have the nerve to ask me that. I'm not fourteen anymore, Tylee. I've grown up so, you can't play me like a child anymore." I was so through with this conversation. He must have lost his mind if he believed that I would go back to his sorry ass.

"I'm not trying to play you. I'm being real serious right now," he replied.

"Do you know how bad you hurt me when you walked away? I was pregnant with your child and you left me. There are no feelings left inside of me for you. You really don't exist anymore. Look, I have somewhere to go," I said as I opened the car door to get in.

"I hope that you change your mind, because I have changed."

I didn't respond; instead I got in the car and closed the door while he stood there looking stupid. I couldn't believe that he had the audacity to even think we had a chance. I was about to have his child and he didn't even care. I refused to let him or thoughts of the past ruin my day. I was focused and something that happened when I was a child was dead and gone. I'd erased the entire incident from my mind and moved on. Some people wouldn't believe it but it was true. For all of the good that had happened to me, there wasn't room for anything else.

I started my drive to the bank and after getting the certified check I went to the apartment complex to fill out the paperwork and get my keys. I ended up getting a three-bedroom apartment. I needed the large space for my office and all of the clothes that I had. It was a terrible thing to need an entire room for clothes, clothes that I'd probably never even wear.

Lisa handed me the keys and I walked through the grounds over to the building where my apartment was. The apartments were more like houses with two levels, one and a half bathrooms, and a garage. I was excited about moving in, especially once I went inside the apartment. You could smell the fresh paint and the wood on the new kitchen cabinets as soon as you opened the door. I lay out on the plush carpet and stared at the ceiling for a few seconds. I hoped that everything would turn out right this time. I needed to be happy and I definitely didn't need any more stress. I just prayed that coming back home wasn't a mistake.

I called Devon to see if he had some spare time. I needed someone to help me pick out furniture. He told me to stop past his barbershop to pick him up.

Again all eyes were on me as I entered but the look that Devon gave them let them know I was off-limits. He didn't even have to speak and they all changed the direction of their stares. When we walked out I burst into laughter. It was pretty funny to me how he had them all under control in there. I felt confident that he wanted to be with me and would make sure that he had me all to himself regardless of what he had to do. He just seemed like that kind of man.

While we were shopping I noticed him staring at me as if there was something on his mind or something that he wanted to say.

"What's wrong with you?" I asked.

"I was just thinking."

"Thinking about what?"

"I can't stop thinking about you. I don't know. It's like when we were kids you were always on my mind. I really want us to be together," he said softly.

By the look in his eyes, I could tell that he was sincere. I wanted to love him again. I loved him as a child but that wasn't anything more than puppy love. I didn't know what to do with it then but I knew what to do with it now for sure. I reached out my arms and gave him a hug. He held me close for a few seconds before letting me go so that we could continue to shop.

I ended up buying all of my furniture from one store and it was set to be delivered the following day. I was so excited and already had plans of where each item would go. After I dropped Devon off, I went back to my mom's.

During the drive my cell phone rang. I looked at it and saw that it was Danell. At first, I wasn't going to answer it but I knew that she would only keep calling back if I didn't.

"Hello," I said dryly.

"What's up, girl? Where have you been?"

"Out, minding my business," I replied sharply because I was in no mood to talk to her at that moment.

"Why didn't you tell me you were moving? I called and your mom told me."

"It isn't any of your business, that's why I didn't tell you."

"Why do you have to say it like that? What's up with you lately, did I do something wrong?"

"I'm not in the mood to play your childish-ass games," I yelled.

"Milan, what's really going on?"

"Look, Amir . . . That was my man from Georgia, okay?"

"What? That doesn't make any sense."

"You heard me right. We were together before I left."

"Well, I didn't know and you shouldn't be mad at me. It's him you should direct your anger at. He came to me and if you were doing your job, he would still be yours!"

"What? You don't have shit on me, Danell. He probably only wanted you because you're easy! I really don't care if you knew about it; the fact is, we were with the same man and that's too much for me to deal with," I replied.

"Well, if that's how you feel, fine. I'm not going to kiss your ass. You've definitely changed and not for the better!"

I didn't respond. I just hung up. I didn't understand why I was feeling the way that I felt but I knew that I wouldn't be able to sit around her knowing that we had been with the same man. I knew deep down that it wasn't her fault but now I was pissed that she had the nerve to tell me that I wasn't doing my job. Who the hell was she to question how I handled my man? I did a damn good job taking care of him. He was just greedy like most men were, and in all actuality it didn't really matter what you did at home. A cheating-ass man was going to be a cheating-ass man. It was just sad how a man could ruin a relationship.

I knew that I should have been stronger and not let him come between us but I just couldn't deal with it. I still wasn't even quite over him but I was going to be very soon. I needed a man who didn't take my kindness for weakness but instead appreciated me.

Chapter Sixteen

Milan

Give Me All Your Lovin'

Devon had promised me that he would stop by with some Chinese food after work. I had been busy all day trying to get things in order in the apartment so I knew that I wouldn't have time to go get anything to eat. Moving was such a hassle and you never realize it until you actually have to do it yourself.

I had taken a break to rest my feet when I got a phone call from Mike. I hadn't called him since our date because I was focused on Devon, so I knew that keeping in contact with Mike would only screw things up.

"Hello," I said, out of breath.

"Hey. You sound busy; how are you? It's Mike."

"Oh, I'm just putting away some of my clothes. I'm fine. How are you?"

"I'm good. I just wanted to check in with you and say hello. I haven't heard from you since the other night. Was I that bad?"

"No, you weren't bad at all. I'm just busy trying to get things in order over here."

"That's cool. So what are you doing Sunday night?"

"I don't really have any plans."

"Would you like to go out?"

"That would be nice. Just give me a call Sunday morning and I'll let you know for sure," I replied. I didn't really have any intention of going out with him, but I didn't want to sound rude or make him think that I didn't like him.

"Okay, I'll do that," he said before ending the call.

Mike was such a nice guy and that's why it was so hard for me to just turn him off. Though I really liked Devon, I didn't know how things would work out, and you always want to keep some other options open for a rainy day. Nothing was guaranteed so I could keep Mike around for security.

Soon Devon arrived with Chinese food in tow. I smiled as I opened the door and gave him a huge hug. He was a little bit later than he'd said he would be so I thought that he might have changed his mind. We sat down on blankets and ate. It was strange eating on the floor but my furniture wouldn't be there until tomorrow. The floor didn't faze him at all. He acted as if he was extremely comfortable.

We were both exhausted so after we finished eating we ended up falling asleep on the floor. I was tired but kind of disappointed that he didn't at least try a little something with me. I wanted to feel him and I knew that he wanted to feel me; I just wasn't sure what the holdup was. I wasn't going to push the issue and possibly screw things up.

The next morning, I woke up and he was gone. He did leave a note saying that he had to go to work but would call me later that evening. I thought that was sweet, especially since we weren't officially an item he didn't really have to let me in on his whereabouts.

I peeled myself from the floor and realized that I needed a bed more than ever. Who knew I would wake up in so much pain? The delivery truck was set to arrive between noon and one p.m., so I hurried to get showered and dressed to wait for them.

I thought about my mom and realized how much she probably missed me. Here I just came back and had already moved away. I figured calling her from time to time to say hello would put a smile on her face. I felt so guilty, especially since the daughter who lived with her was so out of control. I dialed her number to check on her; at least then I'd feel a little better about moving.

"Hello." My mother's soft voiced flowed through the receiver.

"Hey, Mom."

"Hey, babe, where are you? I was just thinking about you." I could tell she was smiling through the phone.

"I'm at my apartment. I'm going to come by and pick up my clothes and things later."

"What's the rush? You just got back."

"I know. I just want to get it all over here before I start back to work."

"Well, though I'm not glad to see you go so soon, I know how it feels to want your independence. Just make sure you don't disappear. I need to see you as often as possible."

"Mom, I won't disappear. I'm so happy to be back. This is the start of a new life for me and you are a major part of it. Trust me, I'm here to stay." I smiled. I hoped that this would make her feel a little more secure.

"I trust you, but I have a few things to finish up here so make sure you stop by tonight."

"I will. Love you."

"I love you too."

After hanging up with my mom it wasn't long before my furniture arrived. I immediately went to work putting things where they needed to be. I was always known to be a neat freak so things had to be perfect. Besides the fact that I couldn't really feel at home if things were just thrown all over the place.

The phone rang and I had to rummage through plastic wrapping and cardboard to find it. Finally I found it under the coffee table. I answered it out of breath.

"Oh, I see you're having fun without me." Devon laughed.

"That's real funny, but if you must know, I'm working hard over here trying to put my place in order."

"I could have helped you but I guess it's a good thing you did it alone since I can use a massage as an excuse to rub you down."

"Oh, really?" I was caught off-guard by that comment. Here I thought he didn't want to touch me.

"Really. I was going to stop by if you feel like company."

"Sure. I'm here and I'm looking forward to that rub-down."

He laughed before ending the call. I couldn't have been more excited. My body was yearning for some attention and he was just the man to give it to me. I wanted to make love to him though I did think that it was too soon. I didn't want him to get the wrong idea about me. As I sat there I debated if tonight would be the night. *Fuck it!* I thought. There wasn't any turning back from this point. I needed him and I was surely going to show him how much. I figured if I asked him to come back later on after he closed up the shop and stay the night with me he'd get the point.

The doorbell rang about twenty minutes later and instantly butterflies were fluttering in my stomach. I slowly opened the door with a huge smile on my face.

"Hey, beautiful." He smiled and passed me a bouquet of flowers. Though it was a little corny it was really cute. It was one of the nicest things that any man had ever done, which doesn't say a lot for the jerks I'd dealt with in the past.

"For me?" I asked as if I didn't already know. "These are so nice, Devon. I really appreciate that."

"I figured I could give you a little house-warming gift."

"You being here was enough." I headed to the kitchen to put the flowers down. When I turned around he was standing right in front of me. Our faces were almost touching. I couldn't even speak. My body was quivering. Soon his lips met mine and we engaged in a long, passionate kiss. I could feel his hands moving down the small of my back toward the bridge of my ass. I wanted him to go further but I had to stop him. I wanted our first time to be perfect. I know that it sounded like a fairy tale but, hell, it was my fairy tale. I pulled away and looked him in the eye. He gave me a look of confusion. I quickly spoke to let him know what I was thinking.

"I've dreamed about this moment for so long and it felt a hundred times better than I could have imagined."

"So why did you stop me?" He backed away.

"Because I want things to be perfect and I know that you have to go back to work. A quickie won't do." I laughed, trying to bring some humor to the situation. "But really, I want you to come back here after you close up the shop and rub me all night long."

He didn't speak. He only smiled and licked his sexy-ass lips. I couldn't resist; I moved closer to him and kissed him again. Before I knew it his hands were moving back down to that bridge again and I couldn't stop him. My pussy was practically dripping wet and I could feel his bulge growing by the second. I allowed him to ease off my shorts while I stood as still as a statue. My heart was beating so fast I almost thought that I was having a heart attack. He got down, pulling my shorts off, and as I raised my left leg to step out of the shorts he met my throbbing pussy with his thick lips. My knees buckled but I managed to grab a hold of the counter to keep myself from falling. I leaned back and held on with one hand while I palmed his head with the other hand to guide him to the spot that I needed him to lick. I was moaning so loudly, I was sure people in the other apartments could hear. Hell, if it were me, I would have probably had my ear up to the wall listening and playing with myself.

As I tried to rock my hips, he surprised me yet again by picking me up and resting my thighs on his strong shoulders. His face was buried in my pussy as I now held on to the counter with both hands and pushed harder against his tongue. I had never had someone who could lick me this good and I knew that I wanted to make sure that I kept him around. Hell, if not for love at least for the head. He was sending me down the slippery slope right into ecstasy and if I could have stayed in this position forever I would have.

After he left I got myself together to head over to my mother's house. I pulled up just as my sister was coming out of the door. She glanced at me, turned her head, and didn't even bother to speak. I wasn't surprised but I was definitely annoyed. I didn't get where the attitude was coming from and the more I thought about it the angrier I got. It was starting to seem like all of the phone calls and letters we exchanged while I was away weren't much more than a façade. She even locked the damn door after she saw me coming; how petty was that? I used my key and shook my head as I entered the house. My mom was in the kitchen washing dishes.

"Hey, Mom," I said before leaning over to kiss her on the cheek. "What's up with Shekia today? She didn't even speak to me."

"Who knows? That girl is going to kill me one day for sure if I keep worrying about her and her funky-ass attitude. I've been trying my best to ignore it."

"Well, don't let her get your pressure all up."

"I'm not, baby. So when are you going to drive me over to see your new apartment?"

"Whenever you're ready, Mom. That's no problem, you know that. I can't wait to show it off anyway." I laughed.

"I'm sure you got all of that expensive stuff in there. Your dad told me how you are with money and I see how you've been spending since you've got here. Just be careful though; I don't want you to end up broke."

"I'm straight, Mom. Broke is one thing I'll never be!"

She looked at me with serious eyes before turning around and continuing to wash the dishes. I was sure that she'd never understand, but it didn't really matter. It was my money and I knew good and well how to take care of it and me.

"Well, let me get my things so I can get back home and get ready. I have a hot date tonight."

"A date? With who?"

"Devon."

"Devon from next door?"

"Yup."

"How did that happen?"

"I came back looking good, that's what happened." I burst into laughter as I turned to walk toward the steps. She giggled a little bit but I used my laughter to end the conversation. I couldn't have my mom all up in my business. Shit, I'd have been tempted to tell her how an hour ago, he just gave me the best head I'd ever had, but I knew she didn't want to hear all of that.

I went up to the room and gathered all of my things. It took me all of forty minutes to get everything together and in the car. Once I got it all in and headed home, it took me another twenty minutes to get in the apartment.

I immediately started dinner. I was as excited as a kid in a candy store about tonight. I cooked steak, baked potatoes, and broccoli and cheese. I remember how back in the day when we were kids this was one of Devon's favorite meals, which was pretty funny, but I hoped he'd appreciate it.

After making dinner, I set the table with candles and then I ran my bathwater with rose petal bubble bath. I laid out a sexy nightgown but after getting out I decided on boy shorts and a tank top instead. I wanted to turn him on and my ass hanging out of the mini shorts was sure to have his mouth watering and his dick rock hard.

Around eight-thirty the doorbell rang and I opened it with a smile though my stomach was doing flips. He looked just as good if not better than the Delmonico steak I'd prepared. I wanted to put his ass on a plate and eat him.

"I was waiting on you," I said in a sexy tone as I opened the door enough for him to see what I was wearing and smell the aromas that were flowing from the apartment.

"Oh, really?"

"Really, so come on in and sit at the table for dinner." I grabbed him by the hand and led him to the table.

"What? You cooked? I didn't think a woman like you would get down and dirty in the kitchen."

"Me either." I laughed, thinking about our earlier sexual episode on the kitchen counter.

"So what did you cook?" he asked as I walked into the kitchen to make his plate.

"Steak, baked potatoes, and broccoli with cheese."

He laughed. "You know that's my shit!"

"I know, I remembered after all of these years."

I came in carrying the plate like a waitress. He smiled as if he was thinking about what I'd just said. It appeared that I had gotten to that soft spot with something so simple. We sat down and ate. The room was pretty quiet except for the sounds of the utensils hitting the plates. Besides that, you could hear a pin drop.

"What wrong?" I finally broke the silence and asked.

"Nothing, everything's just perfect. It almost seems too good to be true."

"Why does something have to be wrong when things are good? Good is what you deserve."

"I guess I'm just used to things being screwed up. I never really felt the connection I feel with you. I don't know if it's because I've known you so long or what. Whatever the case, I'm a little scared."

Okay, now I was really confused. I mean I didn't really know the extent of what he'd experienced in the past but what did it have to do with me? My past relationships were messed up but I wouldn't let it keep me from a promising relationship. He must have noticed the look on my face because I didn't even have to speak out loud before he answered.

"I know that I shouldn't let my past dictate my future but it's just hard. I feel like people aren't always honest and each time I've thought I found the right person I got a rude awakening."

"I know how you feel but I'm not trying to hurt you. I just want to be the best that I can be."

You'd think I would have been the one saying this. I'd never met a man who was worried about getting hurt. I guessed there was a first time for everything. He was still staring at me as if he could see through me.

"I believe you. I just don't want us to lose the friendship in the process. You know how that can go."

"True, but it's not going to happen with us. I'm sure of that."

"Come here," he said, motioning with his hands.

I got up from the chair and set my napkin down. I slowly walked over to him and smiled. He pulled me down so that I was straddling his lap facing him. He moved his face near mine and gently touched my lips with his. I wrapped my arms around him for a deeper kiss. His hands were rubbing across my ass and the lower part of my back. I was getting turned on with each second and had quickly forgotten about the food that I had been eating just a minute earlier. I was now focused on having him instead.

It wasn't long before we were all over the table and remnants of our dinner were all over the floor. It was a beautiful end to the night and I couldn't have asked for anything more at that moment. All of his lovin' was all that I needed.

Chapter Seventeen

Milan

Be My Teacher, I'll Do Homework

The next morning when I woke up I rolled over to an empty space. I wished that he had woken me up to say good-bye. I was pretty sore from last night's activities so I got in the tub and soaked my aching body. I sat there daydreaming, thinking about Devon. Just the thought of the things he'd done to me gave me chills, even in the steaming hot water. I felt good about this relationship. I felt the same way every time I got with someone but this was different. I believed that this was the relationship that would end all of the casual sex and heartache.

Tramaine called just as I was drying off. I hadn't talked to her in a couple of days so we had a lot of catching up to do.

"What's up, girl?"

"Nothing, just got out of the tub, drying off."

"Okay, that is TMI."

"Well, you asked." I laughed. "I got something to tell you too, girl, but I can tell you later when I see you."

"Later. Are you crazy? That's like promising a crackhead a hit. I need it now!"

I laughed at her humor, though I knew she was dead serious. "Okay, so, Devon spent the night over here last night, girl."

"For real? Oh, my God, girl, did y'all get it on?"

"What do you think?"

"I should have known. You know you're a little ho!" she laughed. "So how was it?"

"Girl, it was the best I've ever had I think. He worked me out. My body is still sore."

"I always thought y'all would get together. Do I smell a couple?"

"I don't know. I am not trying to play myself and dive in headfirst. If he tells me that he wants it then I'm for it. Shit, I don't know what to do about Mike though. I was kind of feeling him and I have a date with him tonight."

"Girl, keep him around for a piece on the side, that's how you handle that. Shit, men do it all the time, girl."

"You are crazy!"

"Call me what you want but it's true. Anyway, I have some good news of my own, too. Tyron asked me to marry him. I finally got him to buy that ring."

"Aww, I'm so happy for you. I know I'm going to be the maid of honor."

"Of course you are. Now back to you and your date. What are you going to wear? You can't get too sexy since you practically have a man now."

"Shit, I don't know how to not be sexy. I'm a sexy bitch, girl; it's impossible." I laughed.

We talked for a few more minutes before hanging up. I had a few things to do before going out later. I had to go to work the following day and I was both excited and sad. Sad since my little vacation would be over but happy that I would get back to doing what I loved.

It was around six o'clock when Mike arrived looking and smelling good. Damn, what did I do to deserve two sexy-ass men at the same time? Whatever it was I was glad that I did it. We ended up going over to his place where he had a full dinner, a bottle of Moët, and mood music playing in the background. I was smiling from ear to ear when we walked in, which let him know that he'd done the job right. The rest of the night was just as perfect as it had started. Mike was the perfect gentleman and I couldn't have asked for anything more.

The next morning I woke up at five o'clock. If there was one thing that I hated it was waking up early. I was tired but at the same time I was excited. I was dressed from head to toe in Armani.

I arrived at 7:45, about fifteen minutes early. There was a white woman at the front desk. I walked to the desk and announced my arrival.

"Hi, can I help you?" the woman asked. She was a very thin woman who looked as though she was extremely unhappy.

"Yes, I'm here for Ms. Chambers. My name is Milan Brooks."

"Go down the hall to the elevators on your left and take them up to the twelfth floor. Make a right and her office is directly at the end of the hall. I'll call her and let her know that you're coming."

"Okay, thanks."

I was very nervous as I walked down the hall. I got in the elevator and was even more nervous as I walked down the hall that led to her office. I knocked on the door lightly.

"Come in."

"Hello, my name is Milan Brooks."

"Yes, come in and have a seat. I've heard so much about you. Mr. Waltz from Georgia told me that you were the best buyer and designer he had. I am very delighted to have you at my branch and I look forward to working with you."

"Thanks, Ms. Chambers. I look forward to working here as well."

"Okay, now that we've gotten that out of the way, let me show you to your office and introduce you to everyone."

"Okay, great."

Ms. Chambers was a black woman, which I hadn't expected since most of the CEOs of the companies I's worked for were white men. She was a beautiful older woman, appearing to be in her fifties. She was tall and thin with a short haircut. She was well dressed and seemed to be very nice.

She took me around to meet some of the employees. The first woman I met was Cheyenne Jenkins. She was dressed to perfection, head to toe in designer clothing like me. She was short with shoulder-length hair and a light brown complexion. She seemed nice but looked like the type who could be a bitch when she wanted to. The next person I met was James Liles, a tall black man with the smoothest dark complexion I'd ever seen. His smile was the type that could instantly light up a room and if it weren't for Devon, I'd probably be all over him.

After showing me to a few more people in the office we headed toward my office. The anticipation was killing me. The office was beautiful, much larger than I had expected it to be. I walked in and looked around. It was almost how I felt in my new apartment. I already had plans for decorating. Ms. Chambers stood there silent, watching me for a few seconds before interrupting. "Well, what do you think?"

"It's perfect. Thanks so much. I can't wait to get started."

"Well, I'll give you a few minutes and then I need you to head back down to my office so I can hand you your assignment. There isn't much that you'll have to do today but I'd at least like to give you a heads-up."

"Okay, no problem."

Ms. Chambers turned to leave the office. I quickly walked over to the plush chair and sat down. I could definitely get used to this. I could see already that they treated the employees better here than in Georgia. I mean they treated us well but here I already felt like royalty.

I began to put away the few things that I had brought with me. I had a few photos of myself in frames. I arranged them just the way that I had when I was in Georgia. After a few more minutes I headed down to get my assignment. She was sitting at her desk on the phone when I arrived. She pointed to the chair in front of the desk. I walked over and sat down. She hung up and immediately began to speak.

"Some people are such a-holes I swear. Anyway, I've decided to give you the Saks account. That's not too big for you is it?"

"Absolutely not. I've been waiting to handle an account of that magnitude. I'm glad that you trust me enough to give it to me. I really appreciate the opportunity."

"Okay, well, you'll begin with women's shoes and handbags. You'll be working with Jennifer. She handles women's dresses and suits. The only place that you will have to travel to is New York, where the factories are. On Friday, I expect a full report and price quotes on everything chosen. The Saks team will review the plan and decide on it by Monday."

"Okay, great, so when will I get started?"

"Tomorrow. If you have any problems feel free to let me know. You'll report back here tomorrow at eight a.m. You and Jennifer will travel by company car to the garment district. Any questions?"

"No, you've made everything clear."

"Well, you're free to go now but you're welcome to stay and get acquainted with your coworkers if you'd like."

I didn't stay to get acquainted since I really was in no mood to make new friends. Besides Mark, there wasn't really anyone I felt was worth talking to. Too bad I couldn't touch. Being there made me want to see Devon, so I decided to stop by the barbershop and surprise him.

I entered the shop and instantly everyone's eyes were on me. He was standing in the back of the shop on the phone. He quickly ended the call as I got near him.

"Who was that, your girl?"

"What are you talking about?"

"You didn't have to end the call on account of me. You know I ain't trying to break up no happy home." I burst into laughter. He didn't find what I said as amusing as I did.

"Well, I know I didn't have to but I wanted to. So what's up? What you doing here?"

"Nothing, I just stopped by to say hello."

"Come to my office. I want to show you something."

I looked at him suspiciously. What could he possibly have to show me? He didn't even know that I was coming here. I went along with it and walked back to the office with him. The men in the barbershop continued to look me up and down as I moved through the path that led to his office.

"So what did you have to show me?"

"Nothing, I just wanted to get you back here. I couldn't have them salivating over you too long."

"Do I sense a little jealousy?" I laughed. I thought that it was cute but I knew exactly what he was saying. Men are dogs and there was a roomful of them practically foaming at the mouth outside these doors.

"Definitely not; why would I have to be jealous? I'm confident you ain't going nowhere."

"Really? Don't be so sure of that." I continued to giggle. He moved closer to me and smiled without saying a word. I could feel the heat rising from his body. With force I pushed him back behind his desk and into the chair behind it. Our lips met as well as our tongues with low moans escaping from both of our mouths. I slid my panties down from under my skirt and he pulled his fast growing dick from his pants. I straddled him in the chair and was soon riding him. He palmed my ass and pulled me down harder each time I moved in that direction. Soon he was nearing an orgasm and moaning so loudly I grabbed my panties and stuffed them in his mouth to muffle the sounds. The session was fast but definitely fulfilling.

I fixed my clothes and kissed him good-bye before heading out of the office. By the stares that I got as I was leaving, I knew they must've heard us inside. I tried to act as if their stares didn't matter. I smiled and walked right past them. I heard a few giggles once I reached the door. I didn't bother turning around though I was about to burst into laughter myself.

Before going home I made a stop by my mother's house. On the drive I noticed Danell walking toward her house. I stared at her but didn't part my lips to speak or raise my hand to wave. She looked at me as if she wanted to wave but I wouldn't have returned the gesture anyway. I hadn't spoken to her since the Amir incident and I didn't plan on it either. I was sure most people would think that my attitude was childish but I didn't care. There were some things that I just wasn't going to accept and the disrespect that I felt from what she said was one of those things.

When I entered my mother's house it was quiet. I could tell that she hadn't cleaned up in a few days because the sink was full of dishes. Cleaning was one thing that my mother never slacked on so I instantly became worried. I went upstairs and found her in the bed sleeping. She woke up as I tried to close the door and leave her undisturbed.

"Hey, Mom, I didn't mean to wake you."

"It's okay. I've been in bed all day."

"I can tell; the sink is full of dishes and that's unlike you."

"Yeah, I don't feel so good today."

"What's wrong?"

"I think I'm just coming down with a cold, nothing to worry about."

"Well, I'm going to let you rest. Where's Shekia?"

"She was in her room before I went to sleep. Is she still not speaking?"

"Yeah, but I'm going to talk to her about it. It doesn't make any sense."

"Well, I hope you get through to her. That girl's head is hard as a brick."

"I know. Well, go back to sleep, Mom. I'll call and check on you later."

"Okay."

I kissed her on the cheek before going to Shekia's room. I had to knock a few times before getting her to answer.

"Who is it?" she yelled as if I'd annoyed her.

"It's Milan."

"Come in."

"How are you?"

"Fine, though I'm sure you didn't come to check my pulse. So what do you want?"

"I wanted to talk about the attitude. I'm really having a hard time figuring out where it's coming from and it's really petty."

She sat there quiet, not really interested in what I was saying. I tried to keep my cool because I wanted to squash whatever the issue was.

"I mean, I just got back and we're already at each other's throats. When I was away, we were the best of friends. What happened to that?"

"I don't know. I know that I already have one mother. I don't need two. You came here trying to tell me what to do; that's not the sister I grew close to."

"I understand that but I am your big sister and I don't want to see you get hurt. Even if it means that you won't speak to me forever I'd still try to protect you. I know that I may have been coming on strong, and for that I apologize, but I don't want you to make the same stupid mistakes that I did."

"Well, I apologize for the way I talked to you, okay? I just didn't know any other way to respond."

I sat down next to her. She sat up in bed to give me a hug. I felt a little better about the situation and was glad that we could end this feud. It was taking a toll not only on me but my mother as well.

"Well, I'm going home now. But if you need anything, Mom has the number."

"Okay."

"See you later."

I walked out feeling good about the conversation. I was glad that we were going to be able to put the past behind us and move on. I wanted us to be close again and she seemed to want the same thing. I had a plan and deep down I was praying that it would work. Failing was one thing that I refused to do.

Chapter Eighteen

Milan

Without You By My Side

I decided to drive to Willow Grove mall to pick up something from Victoria's Secret. I ended up buying a long, sheer nightgown and a black thong to wear underneath. Devon would definitely go crazy once he saw me in it. I went home and got in the shower and put on some Victoria's Secret lotion along with the nightgown I'd just bought. I lit some candles around the house and put on a robe just so that Devon would have enough time to get in the shower before he got excited. When he knocked on the door, I opened the door with a smile.

"What's up? I bought some food. I hope you didn't cook," he said with bags in tow.

"No, I didn't cook."

"Good. Are you hungry?" he said, going in the kitchen.

"No, I'm fine."

"All right, well, it'll be here if you change your mind."

I sat in the living room trying to be patient and wait until he finished eating and showering. Deep down inside I wanted to tell him to eat me instead of that damn Chinese food. I laughed to myself about my thoughts.

I was still sitting on the sofa when he came in the living room. Wearing only his boxers, he joined me. It would sneak a peek every time he took a step. I wanted to grab hold of it and get busy right at that moment but I held it together and sat still as he sat down and scooted next to me.

My mind was racing a mile a minute thinking about all that had been going on since I'd come back. Some things weren't a surprise but then some things were. I never expected to be in a relationship so soon. I thought that I would have still been trying to convince Amir that we could make a long-distance relationship work. Being with Devon had been one of those surprises. It was a great one but I was starting to think as he had been a few nights earlier. Was this too good to be true? It felt too good to be right. Was I finally getting the man I deserved or would it turn into shit as all of the other relationships had? I was still sitting quietly, close to him with my head nestled under his arm. He smelled so good that I would inhale until I almost lost my breath. Soon I spoke; I was trying to avoid sitting here with my wandering mind any longer.

"So, did you think about me today?" I asked.

"How could I not after that drive-by quickie you did?" he said, laughing.

"A drive-by? That's what you guys call it?"

"No, that's what I call it, but what would you call it? Shit, ain't really no other way to describe it but that."

I sat there laughing but eager to show him what was under the robe that I was wearing. "Well, I bought something special for you."

"You've already given me something special. What can be more special than what I already have?"

I stood up and dropped my robe. His eyes instantly expanded as if they were about to burst out of his head, and I could tell that he wanted to eat me alive. It wasn't long before I was being sexed all over the living room. It was so good that I couldn't help but scream when I reached my climax. Devon couldn't help it either. We just lay there in each other's sweat for a while until we got the energy to climb into bed.

When the alarm clock went off in the morning I was surprised to see that Devon was still there next to me. I got up and got dressed without making noise. He looked so relaxed and peaceful that I didn't want to bother him. So I left him a note on the pillow and went to work.

Jennifer wasn't there when I arrived so I waited in my office. I used the time to put a few more things away. I wanted to get thing in order so that I could get straight to work when I had to. She came running to my office out of breath at five after eight. The way she was running it almost looked like she had robbed a bank.

"Sorry I'm late; traffic was crazy. Are you ready?" She was out of breath and her clothing and hair were all out of sorts. I was laughing inside though I didn't crack a smile.

"Yeah, I'm ready." I rose from my chair and grabbed my things and we were on our way. For the first twenty minutes or so we didn't say a word to each other. I wasn't really the type to start up a conversation with someone I didn't really know. Though some people would think that I was being stuck-up, I honestly wasn't. I really didn't have much to say. I figured that one of us would have to say something eventually because the ride was too long to sit in silence. Jennifer broke the ice by asking me where I was from.

"West Philly. But I just moved. My mother and sister are still there."

"I'm from North Philly but I live in Phoenixville now. I've lived there for the past three years or so. "

"How is it up there?"

"It's pretty nice. It's quiet and there aren't a bunch of drug dealers and crackheads on the corners."

I didn't know what she really meant by the comment. It actually annoyed me a little because it sounded prejudiced. I mean was she trying to say that she was better that those who did live in North Philly? And if so, she lived there before so she had no real room to talk about it. I probably was reading her wrong as I often did when I had conversations with people I didn't know too well. I moved on to another subject before I got even more annoyed.

"So are you married? I see you have a ring," I said as if I really cared. I was just making conversation.

"Yeah. Me and my husband have been together for five years now."

"That's good. I wish I could be with someone that long."

"You could. You're not with anybody? As beautiful as you are I'm sure you have the men eating out of your hands."

"Yeah, I think everyone has that assumption; that's probably the reason why I'm single. But the man I'm dealing with, we've just gotten together recently so it's pretty fresh. For me, it's at that point where pretty much anything can happen."

"Well, make it last. Girl, you've gotta be creative with these men. Keep them guessing. That will keep them wanting more."

"That's not the problem; they are always cheating. I can't seem to find the man who wants to be loyal. All the ones I meet are dogs."

"Well, stick around me and you'll know how to keep a man."

I was sitting there thinking, *How is she trying to tell me how to keep a man? I know what I'm doing and I don't need any help.* I didn't want to talk to her very much after that. So I sat and didn't say anything for the rest of the ride nor did I talk when we arrived in New York.

New York was great. I called it my home away from home. I loved shopping and in New York you could find any- and everything that your heart desired. I wanted to shop but I couldn't. It was torture and almost like putting a kid in front of a candy store and telling them they couldn't have any candy. I was losing my mind as we went to the numerous warehouses to make the purchases to take back to Philly. Every building we entered was more crowded than the one before it. The hustle and bustle I could do without. Though I was sad to leave the clothing behind I was glad to get out of the crowdedness. There were so many people in New York and I couldn't deal with that on a daily basis if I had to.

The two weeks that I'd had off were now wearing on my body in just one day. My feet felt like I had run track in them and my arms were sore from holding bags on them all day. Whoever said being a fashion buyer was easy was sadly mistaken. It was far from easy and my aching body was proof of that.

We arrived back at three o'clock. I went to my office and wrote up my report for the day. I was finished and on my way out of the door at five o'clock. I went straight home exhausted after walking around in New York all day. I took a nice long bath and called Tramaine as I relaxed in the water.

"Hey, girl, what's up?" Tramaine said

"Sitting here relaxing in my tub. What's up with you?"

"Why every time I talk to you your ass is in the tub? I don't want to even imagine you naked." She burst into laughter. "So what's up with you and Mr. Devon?"

"Girl, if he keeps sexing me the way he does I might mess around and marry his ass!"

"Marriage? Yeah, right, I'd like to see that. I don't think your ass is even ready for that."

"You're right about that shit." I laughed.

"At least you can admit it. I'm starting to have second thoughts my damn self."

"Girl, you better snag that man while you have the chance." I continued to laugh. "Just thinking about a man made me forget what the hell I called you for in the first place."

"It'll come back to you, girl."

"Well, I'll call you back if it does. I'm going to call Devon now that he's on my mind."

"All right, girl, I'll talk to you later," she said.

Devon was on my mind like crack on a crackhead's. I couldn't get enough of him. In the past I had always been known to equate sex with love. It could have been the reason I always fell for the wrong men. I wanted to be loved, and it was that yearning that landed me in bed with men who couldn't care less about me.

"All right. Well, let me go, girl. I have to call Devon."

"All right, Miss All In Love Now." She laughed before ending the call.

I hung up and called Devon at the shop. I was missing him already.

"What's up, babe? How was your first day at work?"

"It was okay, I guess," I said, unexcited.

"Doesn't sound like it was okay by that response."

"It was just a very long day that's all."

"Well, what are you doing now?"

"Nothing, thinking about you. Are you coming over tonight?"

"I don't think so, babe. My last customer is coming at nine-thirty, and you have to work tomorrow."

"All right then. I'll miss you," I said in a low tone.

"I'll miss you too."

I hung up. I was upset that he wasn't coming over. Though I really didn't feel like having sex I did want to see him. I was getting more and more attached the more

I hung around him. I wasn't sure if the feeling was good or bad. I just knew that I wanted to be around him as often as I could. Since there wasn't very much else to do without company I lay in bed and watched TV until the TV was practically watching me.

The next couple of days of work were pretty much the same as the first day. Jennifer was getting on my nerves more and more every day. I mean, she was nice girl, don't get me wrong. There were just some things that I believed shouldn't be discussed with your coworker, which included your sex life. I could tell that she didn't have many friends and it probably was due to the fact that she was annoying as hell. As she did most of the talking on the days we took the drive to New York I would sit and stare out of the window, hoping that she would get the point and shut up. Unfortunately for my ears she never did.

When I got off work that Friday I was ecstatic that week was over. I was exhausted and I still hadn't seen Devon and I was definitely in need of some sexual healing. I thought about calling Mike but I tried to stay focused on Devon with hopes that the drought would be over soon. As soon as I stepped foot in the apartment I grabbed the phone to dial his number.

"Hey, babe, you miss me?" he asked.

"You know I did. I haven't seen you in a week," I replied, sounding like an upset teenager.

"I know and I apologize. I just didn't want you going to work all tired. I was trying to be considerate of that. Had I come over, you would have been up with me getting busy all night." He laughed.

I joined in the laughter. "Yeah, I guess you're right."

"You've been on my mind like crazy though."

"Well, are you coming over tonight or what?"

"Yeah, I'll definitely be there. Just make sure you put on something sexy for me."

"I will," I agreed before ending the call.

Instead of putting something sexy on, I opted for my birthday suit. I opened the door naked with a smile on my face. Devon was speechless, and that excited me even more about the activities that lay ahead.

After we made love we just lay in bed and talked. "So, when are you going to move in?" I asked him.

"Move in! You don't think that you're rushing things?"

"Rushing! Devon, I've known you practically all my life. I've had visions of us being together all the time. Now that I have you I don't want to lose you."

"You're not going to lose me. I just don't want to move in here and we start having problems."

"Devon, if you're scared just say so. But that's not an excuse."

"Look, don't get upset. I want to be with you all the time. Just let me give it some thought. Okay?"

"Okay."

It wasn't okay. I wanted him to move in. Maybe I was rushing things but I wanted to see him every day and I knew it was selfish but I didn't care. Either he'd move in with me or I'd probably keep screwing other people until he committed to me. Some would say, "Commit? Didn't you just get with him a few days ago?" But just as I told him, I'd known him practically my whole life. I'd missed out on the opportunity as a teenager but I'd be damned if I was going to miss out on it again. Especially now that I'd gotten a piece of him. I'd give him some time, but definitely very little. I knew me and I also knew my sex drive and I was bound to stray, looking for the commitment that I believed I needed.

I woke up before him the following morning and cooked breakfast. It was part of my plan to get him to follow my lead. Normally, men would just do as I asked. Obviously, Devon was going to be a little harder to tame. He woke up just as I was finishing. I was standing in the kitchen naked, with an apron and heels. His mouth flew open when he got the back view and realized I was still in my birthday suit.

"All this for me?" he asked, smiling.

"Look, I'm sorry about last night. I was out of line and I don't want to rush you. I'll just take it day by day."

"You don't have to apologize; it's okay," he said, kissing my forehead. "And if you keep treating me so good, you'll see me more often than you can imagine."

After he ate, he showered and dressed. He left to go to the barbershop as he usually did. I called Shekia to see if she still wanted to go look for a prom dress. It had been on my mind since the day that she mentioned it to me. I felt like the least I could do was buy her dress. I wasn't about to let my little sister go out to the prom looking like she shopped at one of those cheap-ass shops in the Gallery.

"Hi, Mom. Is Shekia home?"

"Yeah, hold on."

"Hello."

"Are we still going to look for a dress?" I asked.

"Yeah. What time do you want to go?"

"Well, I'm about to get dressed now and then I'll come get you."

"All right."

When I got there she was ready. I went in and spoke to my mother. She still didn't look well but she said that she felt better. We got in the car and drove off.

"So, where are we going?" Shekia asked.

"To my favorite store, girl: Saks!"

"That stuff is too expensive, Milan."

"So? You're my sister and you deserve the best."

"But—"

"That's it, Shekia. We're going to Saks."

"All right."

When we walked in the store Shekia's eyes lit up. We were looking around for about an hour when we found the perfect dress. It was lavender and fit her shape perfectly. She was so excited about wearing the dress but she was upset that I was going to spend $700 on it. I told her to make her hair and nail appointments and I would pay for everything. She didn't want me to but I told her it wasn't up for discussion.

We bought some Chinese food and went to my house.

"So, you and Devon are together now?"

"Yeah. I think I love him."

"How do you know that? You haven't even been with him that long."

"I know. But I have known him for so long. I think he's the one."

"Well, how does he feel about you?"

"I'm not sure. He doesn't say much."

"Well, how can you be sure he loves you?" she asked.

"I don't know. Anyway, why are you acting like it's a problem with us being together?"

"I'm not. I just was saying it seems like you're rushing it. I don't want you to get your feelings hurt."

"I'm not, trust me," I assured her.

We continued to eat our food. I wasn't sure what she was insinuating, I knew Devon felt the same way about me as I did about him. He was mine and he would be for a long time.

Devon called me around five o'clock to tell me he would be over around eight o'clock. I took Shekia home and rushed back to my house.

I was trying to think of something sexy to do. I wanted him to move in with me so bad. The way I figured it, if I kept giving him good loving every day he would change his mind.

Finally an idea popped into my head. I lit some candles, ran a hot bubble bath, and dragged some rose petals from the bouquet that came with the apartment all the way from the front door to the tub. I called him back and told him that the door would be unlocked. As soon as I heard him pull up I ran and got in the tub. He came in and followed the trail of flowers all the way to me.

"What am I going to do with you? You can't keep spoiling me!" he said, shaking his head.

"Well, you deserve it."

"I don't know what I did that was so great, but whatever it was I'm glad that you appreciate it."

"Well, I'll show you just how much I appreciate it once you get out of those clothes."

I stood up out of the water and let the bubbles run down my naked body. Devon was out of his clothes and in the tub with me in a second. We stayed in the tub and talked for a while; then he carried me to the room and we made love.

The night was so perfect; maybe too perfect, because the next morning was the beginning of my sad times. You never really expect that your loved ones won't be there each morning when you wake up. Even though you know everyone dies, you can never truly prepare yourself for him or her to be ripped away from you.

I woke up to a ringing phone. It was my sister and she was hysterically crying.

"What's wrong?" I asked, afraid of hearing the answer.

"It's Mom. She's dead."

"What? Dead? Shekia, stop playing," I said.

"I'm not playing. When I came home this morning she was lying on the living room floor," she screamed.

"No, Shekia, it can't be," I said in disbelief. My body instantly became racked with sobs.

"It's true, she's gone. I'm at the hospital now," she said, continuing to cry.

I dropped the phone and screamed. I couldn't believe it. Devon was startled out of his sleep by my cries.

"What's wrong, babe?"

"She's dead!" I replied, still crying.

"Who's dead?"

"My mom. I can't believe it. I didn't even get a chance to say good-bye, Devon. Why did she have to go? What am I going to do without her?" I said, letting the tears drop in my hands as I placed them over my face, rocking back and forth at the edge of the bed.

"Aww, babe. I'm sorry to hear that; but she's in a better place now. You have to know that, okay?" he said, holding me in his arms.

"But it wasn't time. I just came back. I didn't even get to spend time with her!"

"Maybe it was enough. Maybe you came back just in time. Maybe you were brought back here just to be with her before she died."

I still continued to cry, and though I truly believed that what he said was true it still hurt like hell.

I got dressed and went straight to the hospital. Shekia was there waiting. We didn't say a word to each other; we just hugged and cried. The nurses let me see my mother before she was wrapped up and taken down to the morgue. I was completely at a loss for words.

"I can't believe that she's gone. I just came back." I couldn't stop the tears from falling.

"I'm sorry, it's all my fault!" Shekia said, crying.

"No, it's not Shekia. Don't blame yourself."

"Yes, it is. If I wouldn't have stressed her out, she would still be here."

"You don't know that, Shekia. We'll never know, so don't blame yourself."

"Milan, it's my fault, and I don't know if I can deal with it." She got up and ran out of the room.

"Shekia!" I tried to run after her but Devon stopped me.

"Let her go, Milan. Just give her some time."

"I don't want her to hurt herself."

"She won't."

"Devon, what am I gonna do?" I said, continuing to cry.

"You'll be okay; and I'm here for you to make sure of that," he said, hugging me.

The nurses came to wrap her body up. I found Shekia waiting outside of the hospital. I was able to take her to my mother's house and convince her to lie down and get some rest. I called my dad and told him the news.

"Hello."

"Hi, Daddy," I said sadly.

"Hey, baby, I was just thinking about you."

"Daddy, I have something to tell you and it's very hard."

"What is it? Are you okay?"

"Daddy, I'm fine. But Mom is gone."

"Gone where?"

"She's dead."

"What?"

"It's true, Daddy."

"What happened?"

"She had a stroke. She hadn't been taking her medicine. I didn't know, Daddy, I didn't know." I couldn't help but to cry.

He just cried with me. My dad really loved my mom. Even though they had been separated for ten years now, they never stopped loving each other. They only separated because my dad had to relocate for his job and my mom didn't want to. I knew that at that point he felt worse than I did because he missed out on spending the last ten years of her life with her.

He came to Philly the next day. I needed him especially at that time. We were there to comfort each other and I think without that time Shekia may not have been able to make it through. Luckily my dad was able to stay for two weeks following that day, which made it easier on me as well, not having to deal with it all alone.

After her funeral I had to figure out what to do with the house. I didn't want to move back but I couldn't leave my sister there alone. So I decided to sell it. I got my sister an apartment near me because I couldn't put her out in the street, but I knew how our relationship had been in the past and us living together wouldn't work either.

She seemed to be straightening out and progress was great. She was trying to go to school and that alone was a big improvement that made me happy. Things were going better than they had been and for once I felt optimistic about my future. My sister was in my life as my friend Devon had decided to move in with me; and I also let Danell back into my life. Tramaine wasn't too happy about that, but I didn't care, because if anything happened to her and I hadn't made up with her I'd have felt like shit. I couldn't lose another person like I'd lost my mother. I wouldn't know how to handle it.

Long into the next six months things continued to go well, but I should have known that it was too good to be true. . . .

Chapter Nineteen

Milan

The Way It Is

Getting adjusted to my new life here in Philly was tiring me out. I felt like I'd taken on more than I could actually handle so I decided to take a break from work. I really didn't need the money and it was starting to bore me because I wanted to open a store of my own. Taking this time off gave me more quality time with Devon, and it also gave me the opportunity to pay more attention to Shekia. I was noticing a change in her and when I confronted her I wasn't surprised to hear her answer.

"Look, Milan, I wasn't going to tell you but I'm pregnant. I wasn't planning on keeping it but I've changed my mind."

"Shekia! How could you get pregnant? You know that you are not ready for a baby now."

"How do you know what I'm ready for? I know that I'm young, but if I can make a child I can take care of one," she said loudly.

"Look, there really isn't any reason to get upset. I'm just trying to look out for you. You don't work, I pay all of your bills, so how do you expect to take care of a baby?"

"Look, I didn't ask for your fucking help, you offered. So don't try to throw it in my face. I can take care of myself, okay?" she shouted as she walked out of my apartment.

I was angry at this point because she was acting so ungrateful. I called Devon at work to vent.

"Hey, babe, what's up?" he asked.

"Shekia is pregnant!" I said abruptly.

"What?" he asked, surprised.

"I tried to tell her that she's not ready for a baby but all her ungrateful ass could say was that she never asked for my help."

"Well, she didn't, Milan."

"I know that! And why the hell are you taking up for her? I give her anything that she needs and wants."

"I'm not taking up for her; I'm just saying look at it from her point of view."

"Fuck her point of view. I pay the damn bills. You know what? I don't want to discuss this anymore. I'll see you when you get home!" I yelled, hanging up.

He just added fuel to the flame, and little did he know his ass would be sleeping on the couch that night. I called Tramaine to tell her what happened.

"Hello," she said, out of breath.

"What's up, girl? Am I interrupting anything?" I asked.

"No, I had to run for the phone."

"Oh. Guess what."

"What?"

"Shekia is pregnant."

"What? Is she keeping it?"

"I don't know, but I know she can't take care of no baby. I bet she doesn't even know who the father is." I was truly annoyed that she still hadn't learned. I thought that she'd made a change but obviously I was wrong. I wasn't about to keep stressing myself out. I realized that some people just have to fall flat on their asses before they changed, and she was one of those people.

"That's for sure. Her ass is too busy running the streets."

"I know; and then Devon had the nerve to be on her side after she told me she never asked me for shit. His ass is sleeping on the couch tonight!"

"Well, that's where he needs to be. He knows that Shekia ain't ready for no baby."

"Well, he can keep being on her side if he wants. That's all I have to say about that. Anyway, what are you doing tonight?"

"Nothing much, my man wants to chill."

"Oh, well, I'll call you back later, girl. I'm sure I'll have to vent some more so warn him that I may be calling."

"All right, girl, no problem."

I hung up and sat there mad for a while. Then I got in the tub, watched TV, and relaxed. Devon came home at around ten o'clock and I was asleep on the couch.

"Babe!"

"What?" I said loudly.

"You ready to go to bed?"

"I'm going to bed. But you're sleeping on the couch."

"What? Milan, I know you're not still mad about earlier."

"Yes, I am."

"Look, I wasn't being on her side. You know I'm always on your side no matter what. I just didn't want you to get so mad and say or do something you didn't mean. I love you. I wouldn't do that, okay?"

"But—"

Then he kissed me with those sweet lips and it wasn't long before we were making love on the couch and I completely forgot that I was ever mad at him.

The next morning I woke up and I wasn't surprised that he cooked breakfast. He was still trying to suck up to me, and it was working. He got dressed and was off to work shortly after we ate. I got dressed and decided that I would go look at some buildings for my store. As I was almost out the door the telephone rang but I let the machine pick up and was on my way.

I looked at three buildings but nothing really caught my eye. I knew that I needed Tramaine with me since she wanted in on it, but I wasn't too sure if that was what I wanted to do. She was my family as well as my best friend, but your family can be worse than your friends sometimes and everybody knows that.

Anyway, I was on my way to get something to eat when Devon called my cell phone.

"Hello?"

"Who the fuck is Mike?" he said, yelling.

"What?" I said, being caught off-guard.

"What, are you cheating? And then you're bold enough to have niggas calling the house."

"Devon, he's a friend. I met him before me and you got together. I haven't talked to him in months."

"Well, why is he calling now?" he asked, yelling.

"Look, stop yelling, okay? I said he's a friend. You're my man and that's that."

"All right, we'll talk about this later. I gotta go!" he said, hanging up.

I couldn't believe that he had an attitude. He knew damn well that I wasn't cheating. He could be mad all he wanted; I wasn't kissing his ass. I mean I knew I was wrong for giving Mike my number but because of the way my previous relationships had ended, keeping him on standby was more of a security blanket.

I went to Danell's house to see what she was up to. Plus I needed someone to talk to about the conversation I'd just had with Devon about Mike. I wasn't sure what would come of it but I knew that it wasn't over by a long shot. Danell wasn't home so I went to Tramaine's house.

"What's up? Why are you looking so evil?" she asked as I brushed past her and walked into her apartment.

"Devon called me on my cell phone asking who Mike was. He must have called the house."

"What? Y'all are only friends. I know he wasn't mad."

"Yes, he was. I can't believe it myself."

"He'll get over. He loves you too much. He's just scared to lose you."

"I know, but I don't think it's over. I'm sure were going to argue more about it tonight."

"Stop worrying, girl. Devon ain't going nowhere!"

"I hope you're right. But, anyway, enough of that. I don't want to sit around being sad. I looked at some buildings today for the store." I felt I needed to change the subject. I hated for people to see me squirm and I never wanted pity, especially when dealing with a relationship. It was best for me to stop talking about it to Tramaine and instead talk to Devon and hope we could move past it.

"For real, did you see anything you liked?"

"No, not really. If I go tomorrow do you want to go with me?"

"You know I do."

"All right. Well, I'm going to go. I'll call you and let you know what time I'm leaving."

"All right, I'll be here."

I left and decided to go check on Shekia, but when I went to her apartment she wasn't there. Regardless of all of the crap she'd done up to this point, she was still my sister and my responsibility. I'd never want my mother to look down on me and feel that I wasn't doing all that I could. I hoped that eventually she'd get it together even if I had to back off for her to do so.

When I went home there was a message from the hospital saying that Shekia was in the hospital and I needed to get there as soon as I could. I got back in the car and hurried there. I was praying that she was okay. The last thing I wanted was for something to happen to her with our relationship the way that it currently was. When I arrived in her room she was watching TV. She didn't look too happy to see me.

"What's going on? Are you okay?" I asked, concerned.

"I'm fine. I lost the baby, so you should be happy now," she replied angrily.

"I'm not happy, Shekia, and I don't know why you would say that."

"Because you didn't want me to have a baby."

"No, I didn't, but it was your choice and I would have dealt with it."

"Well, I didn't really want a baby anyway."

"Well, I'm sorry that you had to go through that, but maybe it was for the best."

"Maybe you're right."

"So are we cool again? I don't mean to come down on you so hard. I care about you and I only want the best for you."

"Yeah, I know. We're cool," she said, smiling.

I felt bad that she had to go through that, but everything happens for a reason and maybe it wasn't meant for her to have a baby now. She only stayed in the hospital overnight, but she was back to her old self as soon as she came home: running the streets and rejecting any attempt at fixing our relationship or bettering herself.

Devon and I didn't have any fights for a while and I found a building that was perfect for my store. I was just starting the plans for the store when Shekia came to me and told me that she was pregnant again. I was upset this time even more because she said the last time that she didn't want a baby. I knew that having this baby would ruin her. She wouldn't graduate from school, and she didn't care. She was keeping this baby, and she didn't care what I had to say about it.

As time passed, I opened my store and Shekia's pregnancy was going good. Devon and I were also closer than ever. Although I missed my mother, as time went on I was making it. I don't think that she would have wanted it any other way.

It was a Saturday when Shekia called me saying she was in labor. I ran to her apartment to get her, and we rushed to the hospital. Danell and Tramaine came up to the hospital as well. It was about 2:00 p.m. when they told us that she had a little girl: six pounds, nine ounces. She named her Jayla Alexus and she was beautiful. I wanted a baby someday but I was too into my career at that point so I'd settle for my niece.

Chapter Twenty

Milan

Maybe This Isn't Love

Six Months Later

"Shekia, I can't watch the baby today. I have entirely too much to do!" I yelled as my sister tried to drop my niece off to me again. I loved my niece, don't get me wrong, but I didn't have any kids and I damn sure wasn't about to raise hers.

"Please, Milan, I have something really important to do today," she begged while unbuttoning the pink jacket Jayla was wearing. Jayla sat there quietly oblivious to what was going on. In her innocence she resembled a doll baby waiting to be played with. As much as I wanted to pick her up, cuddle her, and keep her with me, I had to put my foot down. Enough was enough and I was getting tired of being a doormat to be stepped on.

"Like what? Tricking? Since when did that become so damn important?" I said, annoyed that she was ignoring the fact that I had just said no.

"Please, I promise I'll pick her up tonight!"

"That's what you always say, and each time I'm stuck with her until the morning. I'm tired of you not taking care of your responsibility!" I yelled as she stared me in the eye with a sad look on her face as if she'd lost her best friend.

"I know, but I'm serious this time."

I knew her game and she had more excuses than a crackhead feening for a hit. I loved my little sister to death and as much as I tried to toughen my backbone she broke it into a million pieces every time. She knew that I had a soft spot and she had mastered getting to it. I had to hold my ground; besides, I really had a lot to do and there was no way I was going to work with a baby on my back!

"I hate you!" she yelled, before gathering her things, picking up Jayla, and walking out of the store. I was almost embarrassed as the customers glanced over, wondering if we were going to draw blood, but I put on a smile as if what she said hadn't bothered me. The way I looked at it, she would eventually get over it and I would feel better about not allowing her to take advantage of my kindness. Realistically, she didn't have a choice since I paid all of her bills and was the only reliable babysitter she knew. Without me, she'd be forced to live on the streets and unable to get a job because she wouldn't find a job with a baby her arms.

The day seemed especially long since the remainder of the day was without incident. I was exhausted after working weeks to get my masquerade ball together. For the last three years I'd thrown this event in Georgia; now I was going to try to pull it off here in Philly. The process was overwhelming since I did all the work myself. I had learned a long time ago that if you want things done right you have to do them yourself. I lived by that motto and it hadn't steered me wrong yet.

I smiled as Devon walked into the store around three o'clock p.m. My man was fine and just looking at him walking toward me turned me on. I was practically dripping wet, and had there not been any customers in the store at the time I would have locked the doors and straddled him on the plush carpet that covered the floor. He was carrying a bouquet of roses along with a huge smile on his face. I rose from my register chair to greet him. I wrapped my arms around him and met his lips with mine. I had never been more in love than I was at this point and there wasn't anything that anyone could say or do to change it.

"What are these for?" I asked, as if he really needed a reason to bring me flowers. I just wanted to act surprised.

"Because I love you, isn't that reason enough?" he said as he set the flowers down on the counter.

"What are you doing tonight?" he asked, keeping his hands tightly wrapped around my waist and staring at me as if I were a tender piece of steak that he was preparing to eat.

"I don't know, why?"

"Because I have something special planned for us," he said as he gave me a devilish grin.

"What time do you want me to meet you?" I asked excitedly since we hadn't had a lot of time together lately with the overload of work I'd taken on.

"I'll meet you home at seven."

"Okay, cool." I kissed his lips once more before he left. I watched him walk out of the store, hoping that he wouldn't notice my stare. I couldn't wait until the end of the day to make it home. It never mattered how hard my day had been, he could always make it better. I was sure of that.

After closing the store for the evening I got home in record time. I prayed that I wouldn't get pulled over since I didn't want anything to stand in the way of me getting to the sexual healing that was waiting for me. My body was sore and my feet were aching, but not enough to stop me from getting what was coming to me. I had never been the type to plan out a sex scene but lately I had been so busy we had to practically set an appointment for it.

As I walked up to the door I could hear the music playing along with the flickering of candlelight shining through the window. As I slowly opened the door the lavender aroma tickled my nose, immediately sending chills up and down my spine. I took off my shoes at the door so I could feel the plush carpet underneath my tired feet. A pink piece of paper caught my attention and I made my way over to the table to retrieve it. The note simply read, "Take off your clothes." I didn't waste any time following the directions and after I was naked I wondered what to do next. I didn't see any more notes posted so I wandered through the apartment slowly, trying to find the next clue. Once I noticed the trail of rose petals leading to the bathroom I knew exactly where to go.

The lights were dim and as I entered the room there was another note sitting on the table next to the sink that read, "Get in." I smiled as I set the note back down next to the plate of chocolate-covered strawberries and two champagne flutes filled to the brim on a silver serving tray. I thought, *Damn, he's really trying to show off.* He hadn't done anything this nice in a long time. I was enjoying it tremendously and I hadn't even seen him yet. I eased into the tub full of hot water that soothed my aching body. I hoped that I wouldn't fall asleep and ruin his plans since the water felt so good against my skin. I sat in the water and before closing my eyes Devon appeared with a towel wrapped around his waist.

"Baby, this is—" I tried to speak but he quickly bent down and kissed me, stopping my words and making me lose my train of thought. His lips were soft as silk and I was eager to feel them on the sensitive parts of my body. He grabbed a sponge and after lathering it up with soap he made slow circles on my back. Though he'd washed my back for me many times before, for some reason it had never felt this good.

I didn't say a word but instead let him lead. After washing my entire body he grabbed me by the hand; and as I stepped out of the tub the excess water trickled down my body and formed a puddle below my feet. He stood back and licked his lips as he watched the glow my wet figure displayed. I could sense how bad he wanted to taste me and I couldn't wait until he was able to get his wish. He grabbed a towel from the cabinet and started to dry me off. My nipples stood at attention as he brushed past them. We walked into the bedroom where the bed was also covered with rose petals. He grabbed a strawberry off of the serving tray, which he had carried from the bathroom, and after I lay across the bed he kissed my lips with it. The chocolate melted instantly from the heat of my body. He moved close to me and licked the few drops that remained on my lips.

He began to suck on my erect nipples, causing my body to shiver. His tongue continued to caress them as his fingers found their way to my clit. He made circles on it, quickly causing my already juicy mound to explode. He used his thick tongue to move in and out of my tunnel before pushing my legs up in the air so that my ass lifted off of the bed just enough to create a wider opening. He gave me so much pleasure as he ate my pussy for what seemed like an eternity. After my body shook uncontrollably he knew that his mission was complete. He sat up and as I watched he licked my juices from his lips as I prepared myself to satisfy him the same as he'd done me.

He removed the towel that he had around his waist, revealing his long dick. I couldn't wait to taste it as I motioned for him to lie down on the bed. I looked into his eyes as I moistened the head of his dick. Both of us were in heaven as I enjoyed the taste of his pre-cum running down my throat. I used my fingertips to massage his balls as I licked his shaft watching his body begin to tremble. I contracted my cheek muscles as I moved up and down his thick member and as the head met my tonsils I used my deep throating skills to send him wild. While my throat muscles massaged the head my hands continued to massage his balls. Soon I could feel the hot cum shooting down my throat and I swallowed it with ease. I continued to suck wildly as his knees trembled. I refused to let go and within minutes his once semisoft member was hard as a rock and ready to meet my hot juicy tunnel.

I quickly straddled him and as I slowly eased him into my tight pussy a moan escaped him. I moved back and forth with my hands on his muscular chest. The excitement had me sweating which got me moving faster. I was riding him like a winning race horse and I was in the lead. My prize would be an electrifying orgasm and as I felt his dick began to pulsate I decreased my speed to tap my clit with each stroke. Soon I grabbed a hold of his hands as we exploded together. *Damn!* I thought. My man was the shit and he had done everything in his power to substantiate that.

My life was shaping up and I was extremely happy with Devon. I had always dreamed of finding a man who met my standards. Shit, on a scale of one to ten there was no denying the fact that I was a perfect ten. Devon was rounding out pretty close to the top and the more he put his sexual expertise on me it wouldn't be long before he was a ten in my book as well. I felt like I was floating on cloud nine and when things are going too good you can't help but wonder if shit is about to hit the fan. Though I had always been a confident person I would have never imagined my bad luck with lying men was about to come to play again. I was definitely wrong when I thought that nothing in this world was strong enough to tear us apart.

***

It all started the evening after a long day of me trying to entertain my niece. Yes, I gave in and watched her but little did I know this would be the ticket to finding out all of the dirt that was going on behind my back. My niece had run me ragged and as I laid her down for a nap, I exhaled, knowing that I was going to at least have an hour to relax. As I walked around the living room picking up the various toys that were scattered around I ran across my sister's journal. Now, I knew that looking into someone's diary was a no-no but she hadn't been totally honest with me. Since I was paying her bills I felt it was only right that I find out whatever it was she was doing behind my back.

I got comfortable on the sofa and before opening it I glanced at the clock to make sure I would have enough time to read it before she came home. I decided to just skim through it and read the entries that stood out to me. It took me all of thirty minutes to find out how much of a fake my sister was and how much of a liar Devon was.

After I was through reading I couldn't control the tears that were pouring out of my eyes. I was angry and I was hurt. I didn't understand how they both could look me in the eye when they'd been fucking all along. I couldn't wrap my mind around what I'd found out and I knew I was going to lose it. I picked up the phone and dialed my girlfriend Danell.

"Hello," she yelled into the receiver.

"Danell?" I asked as the tears continued to flow.

"What wrong, Milan? Why are you crying?"

"I'm going to kill that bitch!" I yelled as the anger overflowed.

"Who? What's going on?" she asked, concerned.

"Shekia's been fucking Devon. I can't believe this shit!"

"What? How do you know that?"

"I read the bitch's diary and found all kinds of shit in it. You know that muthafucker got her pregnant?"

"Are you serious? So Jayla is his?" she asked, both shocked and confused.

"No, the baby she lost was his!"

"What are you going to do, Milan?"

"I'm going to fuck her up and she better hope she makes it out alive!" I yelled. I couldn't think rationally anymore, and after reading how much she really hated me, at this point I couldn't have cared less what happened to her.

"Milan, don't do anything stupid! Do you hear me? I'm on my way over there," she yelled, but instead of responding I hung up the phone.

I sat still on the sofa unable to move until I heard Shekia inserting her key into the door. Instantly my adrenaline kicked in and I didn't even give her a chance to shut the door before her ass was lying on the floor. I jumped on top of her and kept punching. I could no longer see her face, and in my mind she was no longer my sister; she was my enemy. She tried to get me off but I was too strong, and since I caught her off-guard there was nothing she could do to stop me. I was exhausted but the anger in me was taking over. I was still on top of her when Danell along with my cousin Tramaine ran through the door and pulled me off of her.

"What the hell is going on?" Shekia asked, getting up off of the floor.

"Don't play dumb, bitch, I read your diary!" I screamed as I tried to free myself from their grips.

"It's not what you think, Milan," she cried, rubbing her finger across her swollen lip.

"What the hell do you mean it's not what I think? You were pregnant by him, Shekia! How could you do that to me? You know that I love him!" I cried.

"And I love him too!" she said as I struggled to get loose, because at this point I could have cut her throat.

"I don't understand you, but you know what I got something for your ass. Get your shit and get the fuck out! I'm terminating your lease. Let me see how well you make it out here on your own. I want you out by tomorrow, I mean it!" I snatched my arms away from them and walked out of the door. They both followed me as Shekia stood there looking stupid.

I walked to my apartment, still in tears. I didn't want to put her out but I did what I had to do. There was no way that I was going to continue paying for her to live there after she'd practically ruined my life. When I got home Devon still wasn't there.

"Milan, what are you going to do now?" Danell asked.

"I'm packing up his shit!" I responded angrily as I paced back and forth, throwing random items of his into bags.

"Do you want us to stay?" Tramaine asked, concerned.

"No, I'm fine. I will give you a call if I need anything."

"Okay," Tramaine approved before they both hugged me and left the apartment.

I packed up his clothes and positioned them near the front door. I waited on the couch until he came home. He looked around surprised when he saw the numerous bags sitting near the door.

"What's this?" he asked, pointing to the trash bags full of his things.

"Your stuff, now get it and get out!" I screamed as the tears began to flow.

"What! What is this about?"

"It's about how you can lie in bed with me every night knowing that you were sleeping with my fucking sister!" I screamed.

"What?" he asked, with a shocked look on his face.

"Don't try to play dumb, Devon, I read her diary. I know that she was pregnant with your child and everything. How could you do that shit to me? How could you do that to us?" I cried.

"Milan, please let me explain."

"Don't waste your time because I'm not listening. Devon, please just get out!"

"Look, I'll leave if you promise me that—"

"Promise? I'm not promising you shit! You promised me that you would never hurt me. You also told me that you loved me and you obviously don't know what the hell love is! Just get out!" I screamed as I threw a small bag across the room.

Instead of saying anything else he gathered his things and left. I wanted to feel better, and even though I was hurt, I was hopeful that things would be just fine. Now I was alone and that was something that I was going to have to learn to get used to.

Every man I'd dealt with thus far had cheated on me or done me wrong. I wondered what the hell I had done to deserve this. I thought Devon was different but I was wrong. I also thought that this was love; and maybe this wasn't love. But if it wasn't then really what was love?

Chapter Twenty-one

Milan

Aftermath

Never Would Have Made It

For the next couple of months following the fight with Shekia, Devon tried to work his magic but I rejected him every time. All I could remember was reading her diary and snapping. I could have never imagined that my sister would ever hate me that much that she'd take away something that I loved so much. I ignored Devon as much as I could. As hard as it was I still managed to do it but then I found out that I was in fact pregnant. I was upset about it because I didn't want anything to do with him nor did I want a baby by a man who had gotten my sister pregnant. Pregnancy should be something that you're happy about but I couldn't find it in me.

I decided not to tell him just yet because I was only four months and I wasn't really showing yet. I was more than capable of taking care of a child alone and at that point I planned on doing so. An abortion was out of the question; I just didn't believe in them.

Shekia had long been out of my mind. I hadn't seen or heard from her since the day that I put her out of the apartment. I missed my niece more than anything and I felt bad that she had to be punished for her trifling-ass mother. So, I was moving on and making plans for my future but unfortunately no matter how much you try to plan things out, you can never prepare for everything.

It was a Friday morning when I received a loud knock at the door.

"Hold on. Who is it?" I asked, tying up my robe.

"It's the police, ma'am!" a deep voice spoke.

"Yes, can I help you?" I asked, opening the door.

"Are you Milan Brooks?"

"Yes, I am," I said nervously.

"Do you have a relative by the name of Shekia Brooks?"

"Yes, I do."

"Well, I'm sorry to be the one to tell you this but she's been found dead!"

That hit me like a ton of bricks. I started to cry. Regardless of how I felt about what she did, again I felt like shit because I hadn't been able to say good-bye.

"What!"

"Yes, she was beaten to death by her boyfriend. He is in police custody and has since confessed to the crime."

"I can't believe this!" I continued to cry. "Where is my niece?"

"She is in the custody of child protective services. If you want to get any information about her here is the number for you to call. Once again I'm sorry for your loss," he said, walking away.

I just stood there frozen, unable to move. The fact that my sister was dead still wasn't believable. All that came to mind was my niece. There was no way that I was going to let her go through foster homes or adoption. I had to get custody of her.

I closed the door and went in to call the number on the card, and the woman I spoke with explained that she needed proof that she was my niece and to come down to the office with it. I had proof and I was going to take it so that I could get temporary custody until we went through court.

I called Danell and Tramaine, who both rushed right over. They told me that it was all over the news. I cried for so long. I just couldn't believe that within the small amount of time I had been home, I'd lost my mother and my sister. It was hard.

Tramaine went and opened the store and Danell went along to help. I couldn't move. I was sick with grief. I was sitting in the tub when the telephone rang. I hesitated at first but I decided to answer it in case it was news about Jayla.

"Hello," I said in a low tone.

"Hi, please don't hang up on me!" Devon said.

"What do you want?" I asked angrily.

"Look, I heard about what happened to your sister and I wanted to be there for you. I know you don't want to see me but let's put all the animosity aside. I know that you need a friend more than anything right now. So please can I come over so we can talk?"

I hesitated for a second but I knew that I couldn't be angry with him forever. "All right," I replied, giving in.

"Okay, I'll be there soon," he said.

By this time I had forgiven Devon, although I didn't forget. I still loved him and I was carrying his child. The way that people were dropping out of my life I didn't want to lose the father of my child, too. I decided that I would tell him that I was pregnant and slowly let him back in my life. It would take time but I needed him more than ever.

I got out of the tub and was just putting on my clothes when the doorbell rang. I had on a tank top and shorts. My stomach was sticking out and anyone who knew me knew that I took care of myself. There was no way I'd be caught dead with a potbelly. I slowly opened the door.

"I missed you!" he said, reaching out to hug me.

"Well, believe it or not, I missed you too," I said, hugging him.

"Look, I'm really sorry about your sister. How are you holding up?" he asked, staring into my swollen eyes.

"It hasn't really hit me yet. I'm trying to get custody of my niece," I said, pulling my hair out of the ponytail.

"Do you think you can handle her? I mean with the store and all."

"Well, Danell is going to help Tramaine with it. Did you want something to drink or anything?" I asked.

"Yeah, just some water thanks."

"Okay," I said.

"What's up with that stomach and butt, girl? You're getting fat."

"I know," I said, coming in the living room. "It's your fault!"

"What do you mean by that?" he asked.

I took a deep breath and said, "I'm pregnant!"

"What? Are you serious? I can't believe it, how many months?"

"Four."

"Why didn't you tell me?" he asked, rubbing my stomach.

"Because I wasn't sure what I was going to do. And I was still mad at you."

"You're saying 'was,' like the past tense. Does that mean you forgive me?" he asked with a Kool-Aid smile on his face.

"Yes. But I didn't forget."

"I know that, but all I want is to be with you. I never meant to hurt you and I didn't mean for it to turn out this way. But I love you and I'm glad that you are having my baby. I guess in a crazy way, everything happens for a reason."

"Yeah, I guess so."

"So, what are you about to do?"

"Lie down."

"Well, is it okay if I lie down with you? Just to hold you. I miss holding you, that's all."

"Okay," I said, standing again. I wanted to say no, but I couldn't. I missed having him around, and I needed someone to hold me at that moment.

I fell asleep in his arms. When I woke up the next morning he was still lying next to me, clothes and all. He woke up when I turned to watch him sleep.

"Are you okay?" he asked, half asleep.

"I'm fine. I was just going to watch you sleep."

"Oh. Well, I'm up now. How do you feel?" he asked, turning on his side.

"I'm fine. I'm pregnant, not sick, okay?"

"I'm sorry. I never been around anyone who was pregnant before so you have to excuse me," he said, laughing. "Can I kiss you, just once?"

"Why?" I asked playfully.

"Why? Because I miss you so much. I love you more than anything. I know I fucked up big time but you have to believe that you are the only one I want to be with, ever!"

"Well, in that case . . ." I leaned toward him and gave him a kiss, morning breath and all.

"I love you," he said, running his fingers through my hair.

"I love you too." I just smiled.

I slowly let him back in my life after that. I got custody of Jayla when she was eleven months and I was seven months pregnant. Devon moved back in and Tramaine and Danell continued to run the store for me most of the time. It was hard having Jayla and being pregnant but I had a lot of help and I was thankful for that.

In September that year I had my baby, a little girl, seven pounds even. I loved her as soon as I laid eyes on her. I gave her a cute name: Samani Taron. Devon was obsessed with her instantly and wanted to take her everywhere with him. I was happy that he was so happy about the baby.

I didn't think things could get any better but my life had always been unpredictable. I was home on a Monday when Devon came in from shopping with the kids.

"So, did you have fun?" I asked, smiling. He had really been handling the father role much better than I expected he would.

"Yeah, it was cool. They didn't even cry that much today!" he said, taking Samani out of the carrier.

"That's good. I was just cooking dinner; it'll be done soon, okay?"

"All right. I got something special for you tonight, okay?" Devon said, smiling.

"Okay!" I said, walking into the kitchen.

We ate and fed the babies. He put them to bed as I soaked in the tub. When I got out he took a shower and I was so tired that by the time he came in the room, I was asleep. He woke me up.

"Baby. Baby," he said, shaking my arm.

"Huh!" I said, turning over.

"Baby, I told you I had a surprise. Wake up."

"Babe, can't it wait until tomorrow?" I said.

"No, it can't. I might not have the guts tomorrow."

"Okay, what is it?"

"Baby, you know that we've been through a lot and we have two beautiful children now. I don't want us to be apart ever again. So I'm asking you this now, sincerely with all my heart. Will you marry me, baby?" he said, opening the ring box.

I looked at him, shocked and then I looked at the ring, which was huge: about three karats.

Baby, are you serious?" I asked, crying.

"As a heart attack, baby!" He laughed.

"Yes, babe, yes, I will!" I said, still crying.

Putting the ring on my finger he said, "I love you, baby."

"I love you too!" I kissed him sensuously.

He eased his way into the bed and continued to kiss me. He caressed my entire body before he kissed it. He took off my nightgown slowly and continued his kissing frenzy. I was so in love at this point that just his touch sent chills all over my body. I turned him over on his back and returned every favor that he had given me, and he loved it. I climbed on top of him slowly and went to work. I showed him that his proposal was greatly appreciated. After our lovemaking came to an end, we both fell asleep.

I couldn't believe that he wanted to marry me, but I wanted it too. I couldn't see us being apart ever again. *Here's to the future!*

Part Two

The Present

Chapter Twenty-two

Milan

Return the Favor

Twelve Years Later

Both of the girls went to the same school. Jayla always did well in school, and so did Samani, but during this time her grades were slipping. She was now interested in boys and she started cutting school. I tried talking to her and so did her father but she didn't want to hear it. I didn't understand her; she reminded me of my sister so much. If anything you would think Jayla would have been like her but she was the total opposite. Why did my daughter have to be the bad seed?

Maybe it was punishment, I didn't know. Maybe it was my fault because of the way I dressed her. I always made sure that they had the best. I took them shopping every week. I know they were too young to be wearing Gucci and Prada but that's how I dressed. I knew that they were hated on in school because of it and because, while everyone was being taken to and from school in bombed cars, they were being transported in a Mercedes-Benz 600.

Jayla never let it bother her but Samani had no patience so she always got into fights. You could tell that they weren't really sisters because they were totally different. They didn't get along at all and they argued a lot as well. I always tried to step in and break things up. Sometimes this worked but there were a lot of times when it didn't. One Saturday morning I walked into the kitchen to hear them hollering at each other. This was normal but the content was different, which let me know what was really going on between the two of them. To me, it appeared to be more than sibling rivalry.

"Don't be mad because your little boyfriend wants me!" Samani yelled, looking at TV.

"First of all, he's not my boyfriend; and second of all, he doesn't like you because he thinks you're a ho," Jayla yelled in response.

"He does want me and I'm not a ho, either."

"Yes, you are, and if you keep messing around with all of these guys you'll be called worse things than that."

"Whatever, just because you're a little goody two-shoes it doesn't mean everyone else has to be. You won't ever get a man being a stuck-up virgin."

"What are you in here arguing about now?" I asked.

"Nothing!" Samani said as she stormed out of the room.

"Hey, Mom."

"Hey. What was all of that about?"

"She's crazy, you know how she is. Same stuff different day."

"It sounded like a little more than just the norm to me."

"Well, Samani thinks this boy likes her but he doesn't."

"Neither one of you should be worried about no boys right now anyway."

"I'm not, Mom; that's her."

I stood there shaking my head before speaking. "Are you still going to art school today?"

"Yes. It doesn't start until noon."

"All right, well, your dad is going to have to take you to school because I have to go to the store today. So I'll see you later and you can tell me about it."

"Okay, Mom. I love you."

"I love you too," I said, giving her a kiss on the forehead.

I couldn't understand how they came out to be so different. Jayla always told me she loved me and she always said thank you for anything that I did for her. Samani, on the other hand, never said she loved me or thank you for anything. I believed that she loved me but she never showed it. It's hard being a mother especially when your child acts the way Samani did. Samani was getting more and more distant and out of control by the day. People were coming to me with stories from left and right, and I'd occasionally overhear things being said about her when the culprits didn't realize that I was her mother. The fact that Jayla called her a ho stood out to me the most. I would never think a sister would call you a ho if there wasn't a reason for it.

I learned just how many other people thought the same thing one Monday morning while I was working at the store. I was alone because it had been a really slow day so I let everyone go home. I was stocking a rack when I overheard two girls talking. I was trying not to be obvious as I eavesdropped.

"So are you still going to fight her?" asked one girl.

"Yeah. Samani thinks it's over but I'm not letting that shit slide."

"I can't believe that she did that to you. How could she be in your face every day and then turn around and have sex with your man?"

"I don't know but she'll get hers."

At first I wasn't going to say anything and ignore the conversation, but once I heard Samani's name I had to say something. I knew that they were talking about my daughter because her name wasn't that common, especially in that neighborhood. I walked over to the two girls.

"Excuse me, are you talking about Samani from West Philly?"

"Yeah, why?" girl number two said with an attitude.

"Because I'm her mother and I overheard your conversation."

"Well, tell your daughter that Taikisha has something for her!"

"First of all I'm not going to tell her anything, and what's the problem anyway?"

"Your daughter had sex with my man."

"What?" I yelled. I was shocked by her accusation. Prior to this moment, I'd never had any reason to suspect that she was sexually active. I was upset but I needed to speak with my daughter first before I'd believe a girl I didn't even know.

"You heard me right. What, you didn't know that she was having sex?"

"No, I didn't."

"Well, you need to wake up and smell the coffee because your daughter is a ho," she said as they giggled and walked out of the store.

I just stood there for a minute, shocked. I had a feeling that she was having sex but that was the second time that I'd heard someone call her a ho. I called Tramaine and asked her to come watch the store for me so that I could go talk to Samani. I couldn't get it out of my mind. I didn't want her to end up pregnant or, even worse, dead. She was too young to be having sex anyway.

When I went home Jayla was sitting on the couch, crying. "What's wrong, Jayla?" I asked, quickly walking over to where she was sitting.

"Who is Mannie?"

"What?"

"Who is Mannie?" she yelled.

"Why are you asking me this?"

"Because he called here. He said that he was my dad. What is that all about? He also said that he was in jail but that he was coming out soon and he wanted to see me."

My heart almost dropped to the floor. How did he get the number? Was he really coming home? How could I explain this to her? I had let her go all of these years believing that I was her mother; now I had to figure out how I was going to explain it to her. I just stood there for a minute, quiet.

"So is it true?"

"Jayla, look, there is a lot that we have to talk about. But could we at least wait until your dad gets home?"

She just looked at me and nodded her head. I was glad that she agreed. At least that would give me some time to figure out what to say to her, because at that moment, I had no idea.

"Where is Samani?"

"She's upstairs in her room."

"Okay, we'll talk later, I promise."

I walked away. That was a load off my chest. I would call Devon and let him know what was going on as soon as I got done talking to Samani. I still had to see what the hell was going on with her and the rumors that I'd been hearing. I went up to Samani's room and knocked on the door. The music was playing.

"Who is it?" she screamed.

"It's your mother."

"Come in."

"I need to talk to you about something."

"Well, talk."

"Look, don't get smart. I am your mother you know."

"Yeah, I know, and . . . ?"

"Well, what I want to talk about is the rumors that I've been hearing. Some girl named Taikisha said that you slept with her boyfriend. Is it any truth to that?"

"No, why would you believe someone you don't know? I don't even know anybody named Taikisha."

"Are you having sex, Samani? Because if you are you better tell me."

"I said no."

"You know what? All this getting smart mess is going to stop. You're on punishment, do you hear me? No TV or phone. I mean that shit! I don't know who the hell you think you're talking to but I'm not the one. Do I make myself clear?"

"Yes, perfectly."

I walked out of the room and slammed the door. I knew she was lying but I had no proof and I wasn't going to sit there and continue arguing with her. She was pissing me off and sooner or later I was going to haul off and slap her. I tried not to hit my children growing up but she knew how to push my buttons and was getting pretty close to taking me there.

I decided to go to Devon's barbershop to talk to him about the girls. I didn't want them to overhear what I had to say. Especially Jayla. It was a sensitive subject and we had to approach it with caution. I drove the fifteen minutes down to the shop and once I got there he was in his office. I waved to everyone before I walked to the back and knocked on the door.

"Come in."

"Hi, babe. We need to talk."

"Come in and close the door. Is everything okay?"

"No. Mannie called from jail and told Jayla that he was her dad."

"What?" he asked, shocked. That was the same way I felt when I heard it.

"Yes, and he said that he was getting out of jail."

"How did he get the number?"

"I don't know, Devon. How are we going to tell her?"

"I don't know, Milan. But we can't lie to her anymore. It's time to get it out in the open before she loses trust in us."

"I know. I just wanted us to do it together."

"Well, what did you tell her?"

"I didn't tell her anything. I just said that we'll talk about it later."

"All right. Don't worry about it; we'll get through this."

"I hope so, Devon."

Chapter Twenty-three

Milan

She'll Never Be Me

Going home that day seemed to be the hardest day of my life. I didn't want to tell Jayla the truth but I knew that I had to. I wanted her to continue to be my daughter and I didn't know how she would react to the news. I prayed that I wouldn't lose her because she meant so much to me. I waited for Devon so we could go home together. I felt like I needed him to go through with the conversation or I'd be tempted not to tell her the full story. When we walked in she was sitting in the living room, reading.

"Hi, are y'all ready to talk?" Jayla asked immediately. I could tell that she had anxiously been waiting for me to return home to get this over with. I walked over to the couch and sat down.

"Yes, we are," Devon replied.

"Look, Jayla, the guy who called, named Mannie, he was telling the truth; he is your dad," I told her sadly.

"So what are you saying, you were cheating on my dad?"

"No, Jayla. I'm not your real mother either," I interjected quickly, shedding that thought from her mind.

"What?" she asked, confused. Tears began welling up in her eyes as I sat there trying hard to hold back my own.

"Jayla, I had a sister and her name was Shekia. She lived a wild life. Your father Mannie made her prostitute and strip to make money for him. And I hate him because he is the reason she's not living right now." I began to cry. Just the thought of her murder hurt like it had just happened the day before.

"What do you mean?"

Devon stepped in. "Jayla, Mannie beat your mother to death. That's why he's in prison right now."

"No, that can't be true," she yelled as the tears finally made their way down her cheeks.

"It's true, Jayla, and I'm sorry it had to come out this way," I said in a low tone.

"So, why did y'all have to lie to me? You couldn't have told me any other time? I mean why keep this from me?"

"Because we wanted to wait until you were old enough to understand," Devon said calmly.

"I can't believe this."

"I know that this is a lot at one time, but we are here for you. You're still my daughter and I love you," I said, reaching out to try to hug her.

"I just want to be alone right now so I'm going to my room." She pulled away, avoiding my hug, before getting up and walking toward the stairs.

"Okay," Devon said.

I hoped that us telling her this didn't change anything. I needed her in my life more than anything. I had her since she was a baby and I never looked at her any differently than my own daughter. I decided that I would give her my keepsake box with all the pictures of Shekia. The box had her diary and pictures, as well as the newspaper article of her death. She needed to know her mother and that was the only way that she could.

When I took the box to her room and told her what it was she was glad that I did. She also told me that I was still her mother and she still loved me no matter what. I left her alone so she could look through it. I went downstairs. Devon was sitting watching TV so I went and sat next to him. He held me in his arms until I fell asleep.

We were both still lying on the couch the following morning when the phone began blaring, startling both Devon and me. I fumbled around the living room until I found the phone just before it went to voicemail.

"Hello!"

"Yes, may I speak to Mrs. Milan Brooks"

"Speaking."

"Hi, I'm Officer Hill at the third precinct and I have your daughter Samani Wilson down here in custody. She was picked up for assaulting a girl at a club last night. She'll be here until she goes before the judge Monday so you can come and see her until then."

"Assault? Are you serious?"

"Yes, ma'am. You can ask my officers any additional question when you arrive. Be sure to bring identification along with you."

"Okay, thank you very much," I replied before hanging the phone up. Devon turned to look at me, wondering what the hell was going on.

"Devon, your daughter is in jail."

"What?"

"Samani got locked up for assault."

"What? How the hell did she get out of here with us sleeping on the couch?"

"I don't know, Devon. They said she's at the third precinct."

"All right, I'll go down there and see what's going on. Are you going to go with me or stay here?"

"No, I'll stay here because I don't want to see her right now."

"All right, I'll call you and let you know what I find out."

He jumped up, ran upstairs and changed, and was out the door within a half hour. I got up and went to the bathroom and noticed that Jayla had gone to school. I thought for sure that she would stay home. She had left the pictures spread out over her bed.

I got dressed and went to the store. Danell was already there and had opened up for me. I walked in and immediately she could tell that something was on my mind.

"What's wrong?" she asked.

"Girl, I had a long night. I'll tell you about it later. Thanks for opening the store. I overslept."

"It's no problem."

"So, did you set up that interview for me today?"

"Yeah, it's at one o'clock."

"Thanks. I hope this one is good today because I really need an assistant bad."

"I know, girl, 'cause I'm turning into a little flunky over here." She laughed.

"You are crazy; you are far from a flunky, girl! I'll be in the office. Let me know when the girl comes."

"Okay."

I went into the office and started doing my paperwork. I had a lot of it too. I hadn't realized how much crap could pile up so quickly. It'd been hard trying to do everything alone, which was primarily why I needed someone else to work for me. At least this way I could stay up on my paperwork.

At about five minutes to one my interview came. She was a young girl, nineteen, tall, and thin. She reminded me of how I used to look at her age. She had worked in many clothing stores before and that was a plus. She was nice and educated as well. She was perfect for the job so I hired her. Little did I know she would be the person to ruin my life.

Her name was April. She started working that same week. Things couldn't have been better. I had more time to tend to my family and spent less time stuck at the store. I guessed one of my flaws was trusting people because I trusted her enough to let her in my home and never looked at her as a potential threat. I should have paid closer attention because being blind will make you lose your mind and the things that you cherish the most.

It was about six months after she'd been working there. I got a phone call at home from Danell telling me that she'd seen Devon and April together at a hotel.

"Hello."

"Girl, are you sitting down?"

"Yeah, why?"

"Because I have something to tell you."

"Go 'head, girl, shoot," I replied confidently.

"Well, I don't know any other way to say this . . ."

"Girl, go ahead; you're making me nervous."

"Well, I saw Devon and April at a hotel the other night."

"What?"

"I saw them at a hotel. I had a meeting at the Doubletree on Broad and sure enough I saw them giggling and laughing and shit. I was going to say something but I know that's not my place so I took a picture of them on my phone."

"Are you sure it was him?"

"I'm positive. I'm going to send the picture to your phone. I'm sorry to be the one to break this to you but I had to. I feel like I owe it to you after all you've done for me."

I couldn't even hear her any longer. I was so angry that my body was stiff. I couldn't even move. After a few moments of silence I snapped out of it.

"Milan, are you okay?"

"I'm going to call you back, Danell."

"All right, girl, call me if you need me."

"I will thanks." I hung up the phone and instantly began to cry. What was I going to do? I couldn't believe that he would do this to me again. I mean, I believed that he cheated but the evidence was never put in front of my face.

I heard the chiming of my cell phone, and as I grabbed it and saw the picture mail icon I took a deep breath. I flipped the phone open and pressed read now. Seeing it with my own eyes was even worse than hearing about it. There they were hand in hand in the hotel lobby. They clearly looked like a happy couple. They looked like we did at one time. I closed the phone and threw it across the room as tears continued to flow from my eyes. I sat there on the sofa waiting for him to walk through the door. I was still crying when he arrived an hour later.

"What's wrong, babe?" he said, walking over to the sofa.

"You! You're what's wrong with me. How could you do that shit to me again?"

"What are you talking about, Milan?"

"April; you fucked her. How could you?" I got up from the sofa and walked over to where my phone had landed after I threw it. I opened it up. "Don't even try to deny it either I have proof!" I threw the phone in his lap. He picked it up and looked at the picture.

"Where did you get this?"

"Doesn't matter where I got it; what matters is how you could go cheat on me with that little-ass girl? She's barely a woman," I yelled.

"This doesn't prove anything, Milan. She needed a ride and I went to pick her up, that's all."

"What the fuck do I look like, an asshole? I mean do I have 'stupid' stamped on my forehead?"

"No, I don't think that at all."

"I can't even speak about this anymore, you're such a liar."

"I never said I wasn't there with her. I said I didn't fuck her."

"Fuck you, Devon, I'm through. You need to pack your shit and go."

"Why should I leave? I didn't do shit wrong. Was I supposed to leave her stranded?"

I didn't even respond. I turned my back toward him and walked toward the stairs.

"I'll leave. I'll be back for my things later," he finally spoke.

"Good!" I responded, still heading up the stairs.

He left. I was so hurt, once again. When Jayla came home and saw me crying I told her what had happened. She was just as upset as I was. Jayla never liked April and always said that she didn't trust her. Maybe I should have listened to her.

We sat there and talked for a while before we both went up to bed. I dreamed that night about so many things. I wished that Samani was home; she was still in the juvenile detention center. She had three months left and then she would be coming home. I missed her so much and it was times like these when I needed her to wrap up in bed with. The next morning when she called I told her about her dad and she was upset as well.

I made it my business the following day to contact April. Tramaine was down to go and give her an ass kicking but Danell was the voice of reason and talked me out of it. Instead I called her at home to tell her that she was fired and that I knew about her and Devon.

"Hello."

"Yes, can I speak to April please?"

"Speaking; who's this?"

"This is Milan. Look, I know about you and Devon. I can't believe that you would betray me like that after everything that I've done for you. I treated you like my own. Even when my own daughter warned me about you I didn't listen. You can forget about your job. Your check will be in the mail." I hung up before she could even respond. I didn't want to hear her response because I'd be tempted to go over there and whip her ass.

Devon came and got his things throughout the weekend and I made sure that I wasn't there when he came. I never wanted to see his face again. He still called, trying to talk about it, but I had nothing to say. I just wanted him to sign the divorce papers because it was over this time for good. He could have his little play toy; he'd realize soon enough that she'd never be me. No amount of makeup or designer clothes could get her to my level. If low class was what he liked, so be it. Good riddance!

Chapter Twenty-four

Milan

Clumsy Falling in Love

The three months waiting for Samani went fast. The day she came home we had a little welcome home party for her. For the months that followed she and Jayla got along well; they were like best friends and I was extremely happy about that. I decided to let both of them work in the store instead of hiring someone new. I couldn't afford to have anyone else around me who had ulterior motives.

It was a Tuesday and I was in the store alone. Four months had passed since Devon and I had been divorced. The UPS truck came at its regular time but it had a different driver. He was a tall, dark-skinned guy. Nice build and beautiful teeth. I smiled as I watched him retrieving my packages from the truck and putting them on the dolly. His shirtsleeves were rolled up and he was wearing a brown UPS cap on his head to match his uniform. I tried to act normal as he made it into the store but he was fine as hell and he knew it. He came in with the packages and walked over to the counter where I was standing.

"Milan Brooks?"

"Yes, that's me," I replied, blushing.

"Could you sign here, first initial, and last name."

"Are you the new driver around here?" I asked, making small talk as I signed my name on the electronic line.

"Yeah," he answered in a deep voice that sent chills through my body. Just the tone of his voice damn near made my panties fall to the floor.

"Oh, you can set the packages over by the window. I'm Milan. Damn, you already know that. I'm such a jerk. What's your name?" I giggled, feeling like an ass for blurting that out.

"My name is Justin."

"Well, Justin, it was nice meeting you. I guess I'll see you tomorrow then."

"I guess so," he said, walking out of the door. Damn, he was fine. The backside of him was just as perfect as the front.

I opened up the packages and began to stock them. When Danell came in she helped me.

"Girl, it's a new UPS guy. His name is Justin and he is fine," I told her, smiling.

"For real? Did you get his number?"

"Not yet, but he'll be back tomorrow."

"I hope you do get his number because you need a man."

"No, I don't. I have been doing fine without one."

"Whatever! You've been evil as hell so dick will definitely do your body good like a tall glass of milk!" she said, laughing.

"Did you order the new mannequins yet?"

"Yeah, they should be coming this week."

"That's good, thanks."

"Now let's get back to this man; how was his body?" She laughed.

We worked until about nine-thirty that night before closing. Devon called that night and wanted to talk but I hung up on him as usual.

The next morning I put on one of my sexy outfits. I didn't look like I was going to work at all but instead like I was heading to the club on a Friday night. I knew Justin wouldn't be able to resist me. Yeah, I was confident but that's what got me to where I was today. I was prepared that day to say whatever I had to. His attention was going to be all on me and I didn't doubt that for one minute.

He came to the store about ten-thirty that morning. I made sure I came around the counter when the truck pulled up so he could see me from head to toe.

"Hi, how are you today?" I said in a sexy tone.

"I'm fine. You look nice today."

"Thanks."

"So where do you want the packages today, same place?"

"Yes, thanks."

"You can sign while I get the packages."

"Okay."

He brought all the packages in.

"So, are you married?" I went straight in.

"No. I haven't found that special someone yet." He laughed.

"Oh. Well, I wrote my number down; maybe you could give me a call sometime?" I said, passing him the sheet of paper.

"Yeah, I could do that."

"Well, I guess I'll talk to you later then?"

"Yeah, later," he said, smiling as he left the store.

I was happy. I just hoped that he called. I felt like a teenager with a crush. It was good though; that was a sign that I was over Devon.

I continued working, and at about four o'clock Samani and Jayla came in the store. "Hi, Mom," Jayla said, kissing me on the cheek.

"Hi, Mom," Samani said.

"Hello. How was school?"

"It was okay," Samani said.

"Well, it's some boxes of clothes in the back that need to be stocked."

"Okay," Jayla said.

"Guess what? I met someone today."

"For real. What's his name?"

"His name is Justin."

"Well, it's about time that you move on and forget about daddy."

"I know. Well, are you staying today or are you going home? I know you said that you didn't feel good this morning."

"No, I'm staying. What do you need me to do?"

"Well, you can go help Jayla for now."

"All right. I'm really happy for you, Mom." She smiled before turning and walking away. She was really maturing and it was slowly bringing us all closer together.

We closed the store at nine and went home. I was tired and after I jumped into the shower it was about eleven-thirty when the phone rang. I started not to answer it, thinking it might be Devon, but when I glanced at the unfamiliar number I decided to see who it was on the other end.

"Hello."

"Hello, is Milan there?"

"Speaking, who is this?"

"This is Justin."

"Oh, hi, Justin, I didn't think that you were going to call me this soon," I said, surprised, with a huge smile on my face.

"I couldn't stop thinking about you from the first time that I saw you," he instantly blurted out.

"Well, why didn't you say anything to me?"

"I don't know. I guess I'm a little shy."

"What? Shy? I doubt it," I said, laughing.

"Well, really I thought that you probably wouldn't want to talk to me. I see that you're all glamorous and everything. Shit, I'm just the UPS man." He laughed.

"Well, I definitely don't mean to be intimidating. I'm actually a very nice person once you get to know me."

"Well, knowing you is what I want."

"That's what I want too."

"Well, what are you doing Friday night?"

"Nothing that I know of, why?"

"How about I take you out somewhere special to start on that 'getting to know each other' thing?"

"That's fine with me. What time?" I was blushing and smiling so wide you could see every tooth in my mouth.

"Probably around six, but I'll call you Thursday and let you know the exact time."

"Okay, then, it's a date."

"Yes, it is. Well, have a good night. I'll see you tomorrow anyway when I drop off your packages."

"Oh, yeah, I forgot about that." I burst into laughter.

"Yeah, right! Good night, Milan." He laughed.

"Good night, Justin," I replied before hanging up.

I couldn't wipe that big smile off of my face. *Maybe this can be the start of a new life,* I thought. Of course, Friday didn't come fast enough for me but when it did I was ready. Seeing him on his deliveries wasn't the same. Now, I looked at him a lot differently because he could potentially be Mr. Right. You just never know and the butterflies that hit me each time he smiled and dropped a package made me more anxious to get to know him.

I put on a knee-length black Armani dress with a pair of black Gucci shoes. My hair was pressed and my finger-nails and toes were freshly manicured. When the doorbell rang I instantly got butterflies in my stomach. The girls said that I looked perfect for a first date. I was sure that I was overdressed but they assured me that I wasn't.

They ran to open the door as I stood in the background. Opening it myself would seem too eager, so I played it off as if I wasn't so excited I was about to jump out of my skin.

He looked even better than before. He was dressed in a black suit, looking fine. *Damn, a suit surely makes a difference.* He looked like he'd just stepped off the pages of a *GQ* magazine.

"You look beautiful," Justin said, smiling and looking me up and down.

"You don't look too bad yourself." I returned the smile.

"Well, thanks."

"These are my daughters, Samani and Jayla."

"Hi, ladies." He reached out his hand to shake theirs.

After a few minutes of small talk we were on our way. When we got to his car I was surprised to see that he was driving a Mercedes-Benz. I knew that UPS made good money but not that good. So when we got in the car I asked. I couldn't hesitate, especially since he'd made a comment about me being glamorous.

"So, is UPS the only job that you have?"

"No, I'm an architect. I just work at UPS to have something to do. It's a good thing that I do though because I would have never met you."

"I guess so," I said, smiling. I was satisfied with that answer and the fact that he wasn't broke made me feel a lot better about taking this relationship further than a few dates. I was already planning to snag him and that made it much more appetizing.

He took me to a beautiful restaurant and then we danced. He smelled so good and was so damn fine. Almost perfect in my book. I wondered what he was thinking, because he had a little smirk on his face.

"So what are you thinking about?" I asked softly.

"That I can't believe such a beautiful woman is actually giving me a chance."

"Well, how about if I told you that I felt the same way?"

"Well, then I would be flattered, but I know that handsome men come at you all the time."

"Well, I have been through a lot with men. It seems like every man I have been with in my entire life did me wrong."

"I'm sorry to hear that. I can't understand what would possibly make someone want to hurt you."

"I don't either, but the fact of the matter is they do. And I don't want to be hurt anymore. I was recently divorced and that's not a route I'm trying to take again."

"Really? If you don't mind me asking, what happened?"

"Well, he messed around on me with one of my workers. Some nineteen-year-old."

"What? Are you serious?"

"Yeah, it hurt, you know. He actually hurt me before that by sleeping with my sister and getting her pregnant. I forgave him because he was there for me when my mother and sister passed away."

"I'm sorry to hear that. So much bad happening to such a beautiful person; and it's fucked up that you let him back in your life to do the same thing."

"Yeah, I wish I had never let him back into my life. I would never have been hurt again."

"Well, if you let me into your life, I promise you that I won't hurt you."

At that moment I felt like I did when Devon and I were first together. I looked at Justin and it felt like I could love him. But I wasn't sure if my heart was ready. I wanted to kiss him but I held back. I didn't know how he would react.

After we took a walk outside and talked some more, he drove me home. He didn't ask or try to kiss me; he just assured me that he would see me soon.

I went in and closed the door. I smiled, exhaled, and rested my back against the door. I felt like this was the start of something wonderful and I was looking forward to what would happen next.

When I went upstairs I peeked in on the girls and they were still awake. As if they were the parents they wanted to make sure that I made it in safe.

"Mom, how was your date?" Jayla questioned.

"It was nice."

"Well, sorry to ruin your night but we have something to tell you."

"What?"

"April is having a baby," Samani said.

"So, good for them," I replied as if it didn't matter; but of course it hit me like a ton of bricks. Just when I thought I was over him something like this knocked me off of my feet.

"Mom, I can't believe that you are calm about this," Jayla said loudly. "I'm pissed."

"Because, me and your father are through and I don't care."

"Well, I do and I can't believe that he did that," Jayla said, visibly upset.

"Well, you'll get over it. Trust me."

I didn't mean to sound so harsh but I was really angry. I couldn't believe that he did it either. She was too young for him in the first place. They would never last. Now he was tied to her forever whether he wanted to be or not. He was definitely one of the dumbest men I knew. I wanted to call him and give him a piece of my mind, but I decided to just chill out. Besides, I didn't want him to think I still wanted him. I went to my bedroom and was about to get in the shower when my telephone rang.

"Hello."

"Hi, sweetness."

"Devon, what the hell do you want?"

"I was just calling to check up on my family."

"You don't have a family. You messed that up when you slept with that whore."

"Why does it have to be like that? April and me are not really together."

"Whatever! I heard that she's pregnant."

"Well, that's a mistake."

"Well, I have to go and that's not a mistake."

"Wait, don't hang up."

"Good-bye, Devon."

Click.

Chapter Twenty-five

Milan

Just Fine

That night all I could think about was Devon. I wished he had never called. I still loved him and I still needed him; as much as I didn't want to realize it, I did. But I didn't have time to worry about him anymore. He hurt me too much and now I had Justin to think about. I was planning to give him all my time. He didn't know it yet but he was sure to find out.

The next morning I woke up and got dressed to go to work. I didn't really get too dressed up because I wasn't expecting Justin to come to the store. I put on a pair of black Chanel pants and a black-and-white Chanel T-shirt. To my surprise at about two o'clock Justin came in the store with a dozen red roses in his arms.

"Hi!" I said, surprised.

"Can I steal you away for lunch?" he asked, passing me the roses.

"Yes, you can. Thanks for the roses. They're beautiful."

"You're welcome. Well, let's go," he said happily.

I left Tramaine and Jayla at the store. He took me to a nice restaurant downtown in Rittenhouse Square. We ate and talked.

"You know I am so happy that I met you. I know that I don't know you that well but I feel like I'm going to love you."

"Really? You know, I was feeling the same way. I have had—"

At that moment he leaned over the table and kissed me and I didn't stop him. I couldn't because I wanted him to. He had the softest lips. After he stopped I just sat there and stared at him with a blank look on my face.

"I hope I wasn't out of line, but I just couldn't help—"

I kissed him. I wanted to take him home and make love to him but I didn't want to give him the wrong impression. After that we talked a little bit more and then he drove me back to work. As soon as I got back in the store Tramaine asked why I had such a big smile on my face.

"Because I think he's the one."

"Now don't go falling in love; you don't want to get hurt again."

"I know, but he's special. I can tell."

"Well, just watch yourself. Because I don't want to see you hurt again, okay?"

"Okay, I will."

"Devon called here, too. I told him that you were out on a date."

"For real, what did he say?"

"He couldn't believe that you were seeing someone. I told him to get over it!"

"Yeah, he better. You know that he got a baby on the way?"

"What, by that young tramp?"

"Yes, girl, I couldn't believe it."

"And he's worried about you going on a date. He's got a lot of nerve," she yelled.

"Don't I know it? Did Jayla stock the boxes in the back?"

"Yeah, she was in the back. I didn't see her leave so I guess she's still here."

"Okay."

I walked in back to find Jayla crying. I walked over to her and rubbed her back. "What's wrong?" I asked softly.

"My dad called again and said he needs to see me. He said that there are things that I don't know about my mom and he wants to set the record straight, but I'm afraid to see him."

"Well, you don't have to see him. And you don't have to worry about him. I'm actually going to find out who I need to call or what I need to do to stop him from contacting you. Now, go 'head and clean up your face. I'll take you home, okay?"

"Okay."

I had to call Devon; even though I really had nothing to say to him he needed to be there for his daughter. When I called April answered the phone. I wanted to hang up but I decided not to.

"Hello?" she said loudly.

"Hello. Can I speak to Devon please?"

"Who is this?"

"This is Milan. Now put him on the phone."

"You don't have to get smart. I don't have to get him."

"Don't play with me, little girl. You're lucky that you are pregnant because I would show you what smart is."

"Whatever, bitch, you're just jealous."

"Jealous? Don't make me laugh. Devon is old news. You keep him so he can mess around on you." I heard Devon in the back asking who she was talking to. She made another smart comment and as soon as I was about to reply she passed him the phone.

"Hello? Who is this?" he said.

"Hello."

"What's up, Milan?"

"Your daughter needs you. Mannie keeps calling Jayla. Now he tells her he has to set the record straight and she's just really upset."

"Well, where is she?"

"She's here at the store but I'm about to take her home."

"All right, tell her that I'm on my way."

"Okay."

When she came out of the bathroom, I let her know that Devon was going to come over to talk to her. She was happy and I knew that she missed him. I did too but I just couldn't let any of them know it. I'd look like a straight-up asshole after all that he'd done and continued to do.

I took her in the house and waited until he came. The doorbell rang about fifteen minutes after we came home. I opened up the door.

"Not really together, huh?"

"I don't want to talk about this now, Milan. Where's my daughter?"

"She's in the living room." I pointed in the direction of the room.

I gave them some privacy. He usually had a way with words that could make you feel better in any upsetting situation. As I was in the kitchen washing up some dishes the doorbell rang. I almost forgot that Justin was coming over to take me out. But it was perfect timing; this way I could make Devon jealous. I opened the door and let him in. I told him to have a seat in the living room. Jayla spoke and he and Devon shook hands. I went upstairs to change clothes and Devon came up after me.

"Who the hell is that clown?"

"That's my man," I happily replied.

"Your man? And you're worried about my relationship and you're fucking that dude. I can't believe you."

"What did you think, I would be alone forever? I don't think so, Devon. And anyway you're the one with the baby on the way."

"So what does that have to do with it? Just because she's pregnant I'm the bad guy? You're with somebody too. And remember you're the one who left me. This would have never happened if it weren't for you."

"I can't believe you said that. You know what? I would appreciate it if you would leave."

"Why, you can't face the truth?"

"What truth? Just get the hell out. Now," I yelled.

He turned and walked away, giving me one last stare before going out of the room and slamming the door. I couldn't believe that he had to nerve to blame it on me when he was the one who cheated. I wasn't going to let him ruin my date so I continued getting dressed and then Justin and I left.

He took me to his house, surprisingly, and he had dinner already prepared. His house was beautiful. I had a very good time sitting and talking so I didn't get upset when he kissed me. I wanted him and I didn't feel that I could hold off any longer so I started to take off his clothes and at that moment he knew what I was I about to do.

We made love right on the couch and it was better than I could have imagined. I thought at that moment I started to love him. He just looked at me without saying a word; maybe he felt the same way that I did. That's what I was hoping anyway. He asked me to stay over for the night, so I called home to let the girls know.

Samani answered the phone. "Hello!" she said angrily.

"What's your problem, answering my phone like that?"

"Somebody keeps playing on the phone," she said calmly.

"Oh. Well, I called to let y'all know that I was staying out tonight so don't wait up for me."

"Where are you staying?"

"Who's the mother here, me or you?"

"I'm sorry, Mom." She laughed.

"All right. I'll see you in the morning."

"All right. Be good, I love you."

"I love you too."

I hung up and told Justin that I was staying. He showed me where the bathroom was so I could take a shower. After I showered I put on one of his big shirts and fell asleep cuddled in his arms.

The next morning I woke up to the smell of breakfast. I got up and went downstairs.

"Good morning," he said, smiling.

"Good morning. So is this for me?"

"You know it."

The breakfast was perfect. I was glad that I had met Justin. He seemed to be the one, but then again I felt the same way about Devon and I was wrong. I didn't want to fall real hard for Justin but he wasn't making it easy.

From this point on we were spending a lot of time together and the girls really liked him a lot. I could see things working for the better and I was accepting it with open arms. My new life was just fine. The old life was in the past where it belonged.

Chapter Twenty-six

Milan

New Edition

Surprisingly Mannie didn't call or bother Jayla anymore after Devon found him and talked to him. I wasn't sure what he said and I really didn't care as long as it kept him off of our backs. He didn't give a damn about Jayla; he just wanted a way to screw with me. I didn't know what he said but I was glad that he did it.

Devon still wouldn't give up on us getting back together, either. I didn't understand why he didn't get the point. We had both clearly moved on. April had recently had her baby, a little girl. I didn't catch her name but the fact that he was playing daddy really turned me off. I tried to forget about him and his "new family," and it was real easy when I found out that I was in fact pregnant.

I had been sick a lot and that usually happened to me when I was knocked up. I tried to ignore the signs, hoping that I hadn't done the same thing that Devon did. I told Danell and Tramaine, who accompanied me to the doctor's to confirm it. I didn't know how to tell the girls. I didn't know how they would react but I didn't have a choice. I decided to tell Justin first before telling them, to make a decision on how I'd tell them.

I went home and called him at work. I told him that I had something important to talk to him about and I needed him to come straight over when he got off. I was so nervous when he came and I knew that he could tell.

"Hi, baby, what's wrong?"

"Sit down first," I said in a low tone. I hadn't even looked him in the eye.

"Why? Go 'head and tell me."

"Well, okay. I'm pregnant!"

"For real? Why you look so sad? You're not happy?"

"I'm not sure. I mean I think I am. I just don't know if I'm ready for another baby."

"Baby, I'm here. I'm happy that you're about to have my child. I wanted this and believe me I won't leave you alone."

"You promise?"

"I promise," he said, kissing me.

"I didn't tell the girls yet and I'm kind of nervous."

"They'll be happy, watch and see."

"I hope so."

He stayed for a little while before going home. When the girls came home from school I called them into the living room and told them to have a seat.

"What's wrong, Mom?" Jayla asked.

"I have something to tell you and I want to know how you feel. I don't want you to hide your feelings or lie to make me feel better. Is this understood?"

"Yes!" they both said.

"Okay, well, what I have to tell you is that I'm pregnant."

"For real, that's what's up, Mom," Samani said.

"I'm glad, Mom. I hope that it's a boy. I want a little brother." Jayla spoke up with a huge smile on her face.

"I'm glad that both of you are happy."

"Why would we be upset?"

"I don't know. I just didn't know what to expect. But now that it's out I feel a whole lot better."

"So what about Dad? You know he's going to be pissed," Samani said with half a smile on her face.

"You know I couldn't care less." I laughed.

We all laughed together. That took a load off of my back that all of the people who meant the most to me were okay with it. I knew that Devon would be upset, but so what? He had a baby too.

The pregnancy was hard for me from the start. I was sick so much that I couldn't go to work. Danell stepped in and helped me as she usually did. I was so grateful to have her as a friend.

I was about five months pregnant when Justin surprised me with a special dinner. He said he was tired of me staying in the house all the time. I didn't know that he really wanted to ask me to marry him. He got down on one knee in the restaurant and pulled out a huge two-karat ring. I burst into tears and could barely speak. I finally said yes. I was excited, though I was afraid. I wasn't sure that I was ready to be married again. But I didn't let him know that. I just acted extremely happy and we were married the next week. Everyone thought we rushed it but what better time to get married than before I had his baby? At least that was the way it's supposed to be done. I felt like there wasn't any reason to wait, and being as it was my second time getting married there wasn't any need for a big wedding.

A few months after we were married it was time for Jayla's prom. I got her the perfect dress. I expected that Devon would be there and I hadn't seen Devon the whole time that I was pregnant. I wasn't sure that he even knew, so when he came into the house and saw me he was upset and it was written all over his face. He didn't say anything, which was best because I didn't want him to ruin Jayla's day. After she left everyone stayed for a little while but filed out shortly after. Justin left early because he had to work overnight. Devon was the last one there of course.

"So, I see you're expecting. I can't believe you, Milan. That should be my baby."

"Devon, I don't want to discuss this."

"Oh, and I guess you're engaged, too. I see the ring."

"Actually I'm married; and so what, Devon? If you had known how to keep your dick in your pants, this probably would be your baby, but it's not. You just had a baby too, or did you forget?"

"No, I didn't; and did you just say married?"

"Yes, I did; and why are we sitting here talking? You know what you did. You hurt me too many times and I hope you didn't think that I would wait for you to get your shit together. I need to live. Justin is a good man so you just have to deal with it."

"So that's it."

"That's it, Devon. And I don't want to have this conversation ever again."

"All right, fine," he said, storming out of the house.

I knew he wasn't going to leave me alone but I couldn't deal with him. I was happy for once and I couldn't let anyone rain on my sunshine.

The next morning I woke up and was in the mood to go to work. Though I knew I shouldn't have I was tired of staying in the house.

I got dressed and was on my way out of the door when my water broke. Fluid was running down my legs like I'd just peed on myself. I didn't know what to do because I was home alone. I called Tramaine at the store and told her she had to close and come and get me. She came faster than I expected and drove me to the hospital. I was so afraid because I was a month early. I didn't want anything to happen to the baby, or me for that matter.

When we got to the hospital they immediately took me into a labor room and before I knew it I was pushing. Justin wasn't there because he was at work and I didn't have time to call him before the baby arrived.

By the time he got there it was all over and our gorgeous baby boy, seven pounds four ounces, was doing fine. Of course we named him Justin Jr. Justin was so happy, I could see it in his eyes. The girls fell in love with him immediately. Danell and Tramaine of course fought over who'd be the godmother so I gave them both the title.

That night Justin stayed in the hospital with me. He took care of the baby all night. When I woke up in the morning he'd sent him to the nursery. I turned and looked at him with a smile but instantly noticed that the joyful look from the night before was missing.

"Baby, how come you didn't call me first?"

"Because you were at work and Tramaine was closer."

"But you still should have called me first."

"I was scared, Justin. And why are you so upset?"

"Because I bet Devon got to see his baby born. That's real fucked up. I wanted to be the first face that my son saw. Instead your cousin was."

"So what did you want me do, stay and have the baby on my own until you got there?

"You know what, let's forget it."

"You brought it up; why stop now?"

"I said forget it," he screamed.

He yelled so loud that it startled me. I just sat there shocked, looking at him. He had never acted this way. We had never even had an argument. I was seeing a different side of him and he was scaring me. I didn't know why he had to bring Devon's name up. I just stared at him and without another word he got up and left. So many thoughts flooded my mind. Was there another woman? Was he done with me? What had I done to deserve the disappearing act?

***

I was planning on giving him a piece of my mind when he resurfaced. Two days after I was home from the hospital he walked in with balloons, a teddy bear, and flowers, and a stupid-ass smile that I could've smacked across the room.

"Hey, baby, these are for you," he said, smiling.

"Justin, where have you been? Why didn't you call me?"

"I'm sorry. I was just upset and I didn't know how to handle it. I didn't want to hurt you or myself so I left."

"But I don't understand why you were mad in the first place."

"I don't know either. I'm sorry, baby." He paused. "Can I hold my son?"

"Of course you can hold him."

This was the Justin I knew and the warm feeling that he gave me returned. I didn't know what got into him at the hospital. Though it scared me, I prayed that things would be different from that point on.

He played with the baby the entire day. Around ten o'clock that night he said he had to go take care of some business and he would be back in the morning. He never spent the night with me, and I didn't understand it. Yes, we were married and my husband stayed in a different house each night. He said it was because I had two daughters who weren't his and he felt uncomfortable. I wanted to believe him because I wanted my marriage to work. I hoped that eventually he'd change his mind about our living separately. I tried not to think too much or act as if I didn't trust him when deep down I didn't. I'd always had a problem with trust and I wanted this time to be different, especially since I was not only his wife but the mother of his child as well. I wanted us to be a real family but I didn't want to pressure him for fear that I would push him away.

The following day Devon surprised me by bringing the baby a gift. "Hi. This is for the baby," he said as I opened the door.

"Well, thanks. Do you wanna come in?"

"Yeah, if that's okay, because I wanted to talk."

"Sure, it's fine." We'd recently been able to become civil and I was glad that we could finally act like adults for the sake of our children.

"I know I acted a fool when I found out that you were pregnant but I was upset. I know I did you wrong and that we may never be together again. But I don't want to be enemies. I love you and I would rather have you in my life as a friend then not in my life at all."

"So what made the change?"

"I know I was wrong."

"Well, Devon, I want to be friends too. I mean we have two children and it's not good for us to be mad at each other all the time. I know I acted funny too and I apologize. But I think that we can be friends as long as you're serious."

"I am serious." He smiled. "So can I just get a hug?"

"Yeah, you can get a hug." I laughed and reached out to hug him. At that moment Justin came in the house. He didn't see us hug but he heard us talking. His face was twisted when he came into the room.

"I'm not interrupting anything, am I?" he said sarcastically.

"No, I was just leaving. Thanks for listening, Milan," Devon said, getting up to leave.

"You're welcome," I said.

Devon left and as soon as the door closed Justin started hollering. "What the hell was he doing here?" he said loudly.

"I do have two children by him, you know!"

"Well, they're not here. So he has no business here."

"Well, he needed to talk to me about something."

"Oh, he needed to talk, huh? That's bullshit, Milan. I heard y'all talking."

"And I didn't do anything wrong."

"Oh, don't try to play innocent with me. I'm not trying to hear that shit. I don't know what kind of dickhead you take me for." He was getting louder by the second. Again, I was afraid of him and I didn't know what to say or do. I stood there frozen.

"Justin, what has gotten into you?"

"You, that's what! Ever since you found out that you were pregnant you've changed."

"No, Justin, you're the one who has changed. Where is all of this coming from?" I started to cry.

"Oh, so now you're going to cry? Keep the tears. I don't have time for this shit. I'm out!" he said, walking toward the door.

"Wait!" I said, grabbing his arm.

"Get the hell off of me, Milan. Now!" he said, screaming in my face.

I let him go and he walked out, slamming the door so hard the floor shook. I sat in the front room and cried for almost an hour. It was almost as if I was cursed. My relationships never worked out regardless of how bad I wanted them or how hard I tried to make it work. Granted, I wasn't perfect, but I was a damn good woman.

After being tired of feeling sorry for myself I got the baby dressed and went down to the store to talk to Danell. When I walked in she knew something was wrong. I was never good at hiding my emotions.

"What's wrong, Milan?"

"I need to talk to you."

"Okay. Tracy, could you watch the register?" she asked our new employee.

We walked into the office. I sat the baby down before plopping down in the chair. I couldn't hold the tears in any longer.

"What's up, girl, is it Justin?"

"He is acting so crazy. I don't understand him," I said, continuing to sob.

"What's going on?"

"I don't know what's wrong but ever since I had the baby he has been acting crazy. He was upset that I called Tramaine instead of him first; and he left the hospital and didn't come to see me until two days after I was out of the hospital."

"What? Why didn't you tell me?"

"Because I thought it was over. Then today Devon came over and we talked. Finally got things straight with him so we could work on being friends for the kids and Justin came in, saw us talking, made a smart remark, and as soon as Devon left he started yelling and screaming at me. Then he walked out. What is happening to us?" I asked, crying.

"It will be okay, girl. Maybe he's going through something. Just give him some time; he'll come around," she said, hugging me. "Maybe when he calms down it will be okay."

"I love him; he's my husband and I don't want to lose him. Danell, I can't stand to lose another husband."

"You won't, okay? Everything will be fine. You hear me?"

"I hope so, Danell, for the sake of my son."

I was embracing our new edition and fitting it in, hoping that things would quickly get back on track.

Chapter Twenty-seven

Milan

A Rock and a Hard Place

For the next week I still didn't hear from Justin. It was a Tuesday and I was in the store doing stock and a delivery guy came in with six dozen roses with a note attached from him saying how sorry he was and that he had planned a special night for us. I wasn't sure what to do but I missed him so I decided to go. The girls said that they would watch the baby for me. They were both tired of me moping around and wanted things to get back on track just as much as I did.

I got dressed in an all black Armani wrap dress and black Armani sandals. Luckily I didn't gain much weight and I could still fit in my clothes. I would have lost my mind if I had to buy a new wardrobe or worry about being fat.

He came to me around seven. He looked nice as usual, dressed pretty casual.

"Hello." I smiled but inside I was a little uneasy. I didn't know what to expect for the night.

"Are you ready?"

"Yes, you don't wanna see the baby?"

"I'll see him later when I bring you home."

"Okay," I replied, though that rubbed me the wrong way. He hadn't seen him in a week and didn't seem at all interested in him. That wasn't a good sign or a good way to start the night.

The rest of our date was actually pretty nice. We went on a horse and carriage ride through the city and then went to a nice quiet restaurant to eat. It was nice but the whole time we never talked about the way that he acted. I didn't want to bring it up but it was definitely on my mind.

After we ate he took me home. He came in to see the baby for a minute and then he kissed me good-bye and left. I was glad that he was acting civil but he still wasn't the same. Something was going on that I didn't know about. I decided that it was best not to press the issue because that hadn't worked out well in the past. I was hoping that we'd get back to the way we were in the beginning, and in the weeks that followed he started to get back to normal.

Jayla's graduation came next. I was ecstatic that she was graduating, though I never doubted that she would. She was going to the Fashion Institute of Technology in New York. She wanted to follow in my footsteps, which was great because people always needed clothes, so to me that was a guaranteed money maker. She was going to stay on campus. At first I didn't want her to but I had to let her go. They were growing up and I really was taking it hard now that I had another little baby.

On her graduation day Justin wasn't able to make it, but he gave me a card with money in it to give to her as a gift. I was a little upset that he wasn't going to share that day with me but I'd learned in the past not to press things with him so I just kept quiet. Devon was there, rightfully so, and he chose to sit next to me at the ceremony.

"She's beautiful isn't she?" he leaned over to me and whispered.

"I know. I'm so glad she's graduating."

"I am too. Here let me hold the baby."

I gave him a strange look but then I loosened up and agreed. "Okay." I passed him the baby.

"So, how have you been?"

"Fine, I went back to work."

"That's good, I didn't know. I bet you were glad. Being cooped up in the house ain't like you. Maybe I'll stop by sometimes if that's okay?"

"Yeah, that would be nice." I smiled.

"Cool."

Devon was surprising me more and more. He was playing with my son and at first he was so upset that I was having another man's child. I still loved Devon but I didn't want to be with him. I wanted Justin.

After the graduation we all went to Red Lobster to eat. Devon came along. It was actually fun. That night Justin came over when I was putting the baby to sleep.

"Hi. How was the graduation?"

"It was nice."

"That's good. How's the baby?"

"He's fine."

"Why all the short-ass answers tonight?"

"Justin, please don't start."

"Don't tell me what the hell to do. I asked you a question!"

"Nothing, Justin. I'm just tired. I have a newborn baby who keeps me up all night. I guess you wouldn't know because you're never here."

"What did you say?"

"Nothing, Justin. Forget it."

"I said what did you say!" he said, grabbing my arm tightly.

"Justin, you're hurting my arm."

"I don't care. What the fuck did you say?"

"Calm down; you're going to wake the girls up."

"I told you not to tell me what to do, didn't I?"

"Justin," I screamed.

"Fuck you, okay?" he said as he spit in my face and walked toward the door.

I broke down as I wiped his spit from my face. I had never been so disrespected in my entire life. I was sitting down sobbing when the girls came running into the room after they heard him leave.

"Mom, are you okay?" Jayla asked.

"Yes, I'm fine."

"Did he hit you?" Samani was visibly angry.

"No, he didn't. I'm fine, okay? You girls go back to bed, okay? I'll be fine."

"Mom, you can't keep letting him get away with acting like that."

"Jayla, I'm fine. I can take care of myself, okay? Now go back to bed. This conversation is over."

They both looked at me with anger. Jayla sucked her teeth before leaving the room. As soon as I heard their room doors close I burst into tears. Why me, why was this happening to me? Our entire relationship had been fine up to this point. What had I done to deserve this? Was I ever going to get a good man? Devon treated me bad but not in this way. He'd never disrespected me the way Justin had. At this point I was so afraid of Justin, and his anger was only escalating, which to me meant hitting was next.

I called Danell on the phone. I needed a friend who could listen and be a shoulder for me.

"Hello?"

"Danell, he spit in my face," I blurted out.

"He did what?"

"He yelled at me, cussed at me, and then spit in my face."

"What? Do you need me to come over there?"

"No, I'm okay."

"Are you sure?"

"I'm sure. He's not going to come back. I don't know what to do, Danell."

"It's time you make a decision because this relationship is not healthy, and next thing you know he's going to be knocking you upside the head."

"I don't think he'd hit me," I responded trying to sugar coat it.

"Are you kidding me? That's the only thing left. He just degraded you by spitting in your face."

"I know. Look, the baby's crying. I'll call you in the morning, okay?" I quickly ended the conversation because I was starting to feel sorry for myself again.

"Okay. Make sure you call me if he comes back acting up."

"I will. Good night."

I hung up the phone. At that moment I started to think about my sister and what happened to her. Could Justin turn out like Mannie? I was so afraid that I decided to call Devon. I knew that it may have been a mistake but I felt like he should know what was going on, since his children were witnessing these outbursts that Justin had been having.

"Hello."

"Hello, can I speak to Devon please?"

"Who's calling?" April replied.

"Milan."

"Hold on," she said without a smart remark for once.

"Hello."

"Devon, I need you to come over here please."

"What's wrong, are the girls okay?"

"Yes, but I'm not. Please could you come over?"

"I'll be there in a few, all right?"

"All right, I'll be downstairs waiting."

"Okay."

He got there about twenty minutes later. I still had tear tracks running down my face.

"What's wrong?"

"It's Justin. I don't know what's wrong with him."

"What's going on? Did he hit you?"

"The day after I had the baby, we had an argument because I didn't call him first to come and get me; then I didn't see or hear from him for two days. Then that day that you were over here we argued because I was talking to you, and then he disappeared for a week. Tonight he came over and just blew up for nothing and then he spit in my face and walked out."

"So he didn't hit you?"

"No, he didn't. But I'm scared. I feel like that's next," I cried.

"Well, do you want him back?"

"I don't know."

"Well, why did you call me?"

"Because I need you," I said honestly.

"But why would—"

Without warning I kissed him. I didn't know what came over me but whatever it was it felt good. I missed him so much and he didn't push me away like I expected; he just followed my lead. Soon I was undressing and working toward undressing him.

"Milan, are you sure you want to do this?"

"Devon, I want you." I continued to tug at his clothing.

We made love right in the living room. I wasn't sure why I did what I did but as soon as it was over I felt guilty. I was still married to Justin so technically I was cheating. I hadn't even thought about what would happen afterward.

We didn't say anything to each other. He kissed me good-bye and left. I went to bed that night confused.

For the next couple of weeks I didn't hear from Justin. I tried to reach him often to no avail. Even the numerous voicemails didn't get a response. He didn't even come see the baby. My child was almost three months old and I could only remember Justin holding him four times. It's like he didn't care about him. I tried not to let it break me down even more than it already had. Whatever was meant to be would be and obviously this marriage to Justin wasn't the match made in heaven that I once thought it was. I could definitely see a divorce brewing. I was getting sick of calling and begging him as if I'd done something to him. I didn't deserve it and I was almost at the brink of throwing in the towel.

In the months that followed not much changed. Jayla was on her way off to college and I dreaded watching her go. Devon kept coming around but we didn't sleep together, and instead we just talked. I was still holding on to the relationship with Justin even though he often did a disappearing act. Talking to Devon was actually giving me hope that there was something better for me and I needed to just cut ties with Justin. Regardless of how bad I wanted to kick him to the curb, he always found a way to get on my good side somehow. This time it was over a phone call.

"Hello?" I picked up the phone holding the baby in my arms.

"Hi," he responded dryly.

"What do you want, Justin?" I yelled.

"Now why you do you have to act like that, Milan?"

"Because I haven't heard from you and I'm tired of this shit, Justin. I can seriously do bad by my damn self."

"I know, and I'm sorry. Is it okay if I come over so we can talk?"

"Anything you have to say to me you can say it now; otherwise, we don't have shit to talk about."

"I am truly sorry and I miss you. I promised you that I would never hurt you and that's exactly what I did. I was wrong and I need you in my life more than ever. I can't live without you."

"Well, you should have thought about that before you spit in my face. And obviously you can live without me because you've done well the past four and a half months."

"I'm sorry about that."

"That's all you have to say is sorry? When someone is sorry they don't do the same shit repeatedly. This is a pattern for you. "

"I am really sorry and I mean it. I wouldn't be calling you if I didn't care for you."

"So what are you asking me?"

"To accept my apology and give me a chance to make things right," he responded in that soothing tone that usually got me to change my mind.

"You can't be serious, Justin."

"I am very serious, Milan. I wouldn't have called you if I didn't want to be with you."

"I'm not ready to be with you now. I can't trust that the next time you get upset you won't really hurt me. You can't possibly really want me; you don't even care about your child."

"Yes, I do. I love him."

"You have only held him four times since he's been born, Justin. Four."

"I know and I want to be more involved in his life. You just have to be with me."

"You don't need to be with me to be in his life."

"So what are you saying, Milan?"

"I'm saying you have to give me some time, that's all. But your son needs you now."

"I understand that. So when can I come and see him?"

"How about tomorrow, Justin?"

"Okay, I'll call you tomorrow then."

"Okay. Good-bye, Justin."

"Not good-bye. See you later."

I just hung up. I was still angry and I was going to need more of an explanation once we were face to face. I needed to look him in the eye and hopefully see through his bullshit if he was lying. Devon and I had been reconnecting and being alone wasn't something that I enjoyed. He was being the friend I had long ago, the friend who was always there for me. Regardless of the way I felt I had to figure out where things stood with Justin before I could even think of starting something with Devon. I wasn't trying to lead Devon on in any way but I wanted to keep him around as a friend as long as I could.

I didn't know how he got the impression that we were getting back together but when he saw that Justin started coming around he was upset. I couldn't say that I was surprised but I'd somehow hoped that he would understand the position that I was in.

"Why is he coming around again?" he yelled.

"Because he needs to see his son. What's the problem, Devon?"

"His son wasn't that important to him when he disappeared for all that time. He doesn't care about you and you're crazy if you let him back in your life."

"So why were you an exception? At least he didn't sleep around on me. I let you back in my life."

"But that was different."

"How was it different? You both hurt me."

"Well, like I said, you're crazy. I love you, and you gave me the impression that we might get back together, and that's wrong if you were just using me to fill his spot until he came back around. If that's all you wanted just don't come running to me to pick up the pieces when your world crumbles."

"Devon, it doesn't have to be that way. I didn't use you. I needed a friend and you were there. I thank you for everything that you have done for me and I love you too. But he's my husband."

"I don't want to hear that shit, Milan. I know he's your husband but I was your husband too. What does that mean, nothing? I was the one who was there for you when anything bad happened. I left my woman, argued, and fought because you needed me. I didn't throw it in your face. It's up to you how you want this to be. Just know that I won't always be here when you need a shoulder to cry on."

"But I don't understand. How come we can't just be friends?"

"Because it's not that easy for me. I know that I hurt you. I know I was wrong for everything I did but at one point in time we were together. Not friends. I think the world of you; and to show you how much he cares, he spit in your face like you were trash. How could you want him back, Milan? Just give me one good reason and I'll accept it."

"Devon, I can't explain it, but the fact is I love him and he's my husband. It's just as simple as that."

"Well, if that's how it's going to be, just remember what I said. Tell my daughters I love them and if they want to talk to me they can call me at home or at the shop."

"Devon, wait!"

"That's it, Milan. I'm done. I'll see you around."

He turned and walked out on me. I was sad but I couldn't cry. Maybe it was best. I knew that Justin and I wouldn't work with Devon hanging around anyway so that was a sacrifice I was going to have to make. I wanted my life back, the life I had with Justin before all of the drama, and each day that passed I could see it happening. The rock and a hard place I was stuck between were slowly releasing me. I knew who I wanted to be with and I planned to do just that.

Chapter Twenty-eight

Milan

Again

As time went on Justin and I were getting closer. He still hadn't moved in but he was coming around much more often. I missed all his love. He was spending a lot of time with the baby and me and I was happy again. Things with Jayla and school were great but at home Samani was acting weird. I tried not to overthink it and tried to give her the benefit of the doubt. Rather than assume, I waited, and soon enough I found out exactly what the issue was. One day at the store she was working with me. It was about six o'clock and I figured I'd bring it up to see what she'd say. I hoped that she would be honest but honesty wasn't always a trait that she'd possessed in the past.

"So, Samani, what's been going on with you lately?"

"What do you mean? I'm fine."

"You don't seem fine. You've been distant lately."

"Nothing is wrong, Mom, I'm okay. I've just been a little under the weather."

"Okay. I'll leave it alone."

She got up to put some boxes away and as she lifted the boxes up she fainted. I ran over to her and when she didn't respond, I rushed her to the hospital.

We were in the emergency room for four hours before the doctor told me what was wrong. She was pregnant and I should have known. History was repeating itself for sure. When the doctor told me I was shocked but even more shocked to find out that she had been taking various drugs to try to kill the baby. Why would she try to kill the baby? She could have killed herself. If getting rid of the baby was what she wanted I would have taken her to get an abortion.

Once I was allowed into the room I went in to find her sleeping, I just stared at her. This was my little baby who was becoming a woman. She was almost finished with her twelfth grade year at least. I couldn't be mad at her when I did the same thing as a teenager. Luckily my mother caught on quick enough to nip it in the bud and help me move on with my life. I sat there thinking of how devastated I would have been to lose her and I wondered why she felt like she couldn't talk to me. I thought that I had always been easy to talk to. I hadn't called Devon yet because I didn't know what to tell him. As I sat down in the chair she woke up. Turning over and noticing me in the chair.

"Hi, baby, how do you feel?"

"Mom, I'm sorry, okay? I didn't want you to find out this way. I wanted to get an abortion but I was afraid to come to you." She immediately began speaking out. I wasn't even angry. I was just glad that she was okay.

"You know that you can talk to me about anything. I am a little upset that you're pregnant but most of all that you tried to hurt yourself. I don't know what I would do if I lost you."

"Mom, I'm sorry. Did you tell Dad yet?"

"No, but I am. I was about to tell him soon."

"Well, could you just tell him to come here and I'll tell him myself."

"Yeah, I'll go call him now."

"Okay. Thanks, Mom, for being understanding."

"That's what moms are for." I smiled as I walked toward the door.

I went out in the lobby and called Devon. I wasn't surprised when April answered the phone.

"Hello."

"Hi, could I speak to Devon?"

"Milan, he doesn't want to talk to you."

"What! Put him on the phone; this does not concern you."

"Yes, it does. He doesn't want to talk. What part don't you understand?"

"Look, bitch, my daughter is in the hospital and I think he needs to know, okay?"

"Devon, get the phone," she said angrily.

"Hello," he said loudly.

"Oh, so you don't want to talk to me now?"

"Milan, what is it?"

"Your daughter is in the hospital, okay? And she needs you."

"What's wrong?"

"She wants to tell you herself, so could you come up here as soon as possible? We're at Temple."

"All right, I'll be there."

He had the nerve to bring April. I knew that he was trying to make me jealous, but this was unnecessary and I had to say something.

"Why did you bring that bitch?"

"Look, I'm not going to be too many of your bitches," April yelled.

"Whatever. Devon, how could you bring her up here?"

"Because she's my woman. Now where's my daughter?"

"Well, was she your woman when you made love to me?"

"Huh? What is this bitch talking about?"

"Now why did you have to go there?" he said loudly.

"What the hell is she talking about, Devon?"

"I'm talking about the fact that he made love to me."

"Devon, is this true?"

"We'll talk about it later."

"I said is it true?" she screamed.

"Wait until we get home, okay?"

"All right, I'll wait, all right."

"Where's my daughter?"

"The last room on the left."

I tried not to laugh. I was glad that I had gotten that off my chest. She needed to know. I followed him in the room. April stayed out in the lobby. When I walked in he was hugging Samani.

"So what's going on, are you okay?" He sat down in the chair.

"Daddy, I'm pregnant."

"What?"

"I'm pregnant."

"So why are you in here?"

"Because I tried to kill it. Daddy, I'm sorry if I disappointed you in any way."

"You didn't disappoint me. I love you. I'm here for you no matter what, okay?"

"Okay."

"Now I need to talk to your mother but I'll be here in the morning to see you, okay?" he said, kissing her on the cheek.

"Okay."

We walked out into the hallway. I knew what he wanted. Immediately he began yelling at me, which was what I expected he'd do.

"What the hell was that about?"

"You shouldn't have brought that tramp in here, Devon. That was real disrespectful."

"Milan, you said plainly that you didn't want me so why are you upset that I am with her? She is the mother of my child."

"Okay, but you didn't have to bring her here."

"Now I have to go home and explain this shit!"

"Well, good luck!"

"Good luck? If you had never played with my heart this wouldn't have happened."

"That's not true, Devon."

"You know what? I don't wanna talk about this. I have to go home, okay?"

"Fine!"

He was mad at me and I couldn't care less. I went back in the room and Samani had fallen asleep that fast. I called Danell and asked her to keep Justin for me because I wasn't coming home.

I stayed in the hospital all night. When I woke up Samani was still asleep. She woke up when I came back from getting some coffee.

"Hey, sweetie!"

"Hey, Mom. I can't believe you stayed here all night. What were you and Dad arguing about last night?"

"Nothing as usual."

"Oh. Am I going home today?"

"I believe so. I'll go ask the nurse, okay?"

"Okay."

As I walked out Devon was coming down the hall. He still looked upset but at least he was alone.

"How is she?"

"She's better. I'm going to find out if she's going home today or not."

"All right, I'll go in."

"Okay."

I couldn't believe that he was acting civil as if he had forgotten about last night. April must have forgiven him. I went to the nurses' station to find out about her leaving and they told me that she would be discharged that day. Devon said he would bring her home so I went home to get the baby from Danell.

When I came in the house Justin Jr. ran into my arms. "Hey, baby," I said, picking him up.

"He actually slept all night, do you believe it?" Danell said, smiling.

"For real, he won't do that for me. Girl, you know Devon had the nerve to bring April with him to the hospital last night?"

"He did what? I can't believe he would do that."

"He sure did. That's why I told her that we slept together."

"Girl, you are so crazy. I know he was mad." She laughed.

"He sure was. Did Justin call?"

"No, but some woman named Tracey did. She said she needed to talk to you about Justin. She left her number."

"Okay, I'll call her tonight."

Danell left shortly after that. It was Sunday so the store was closed. I washed the baby and put him down for a nap. *Tracey?* I wondered what she could possibly have to tell me about Justin. The way things had been going I hoped that it wasn't anything horrible; however, an unknown woman calling about my husband certainly couldn't be good news.

I found the number on the counter and dialed it, bracing myself for the conversation. After two rings a woman answered the phone.

"Hello."

"Hi, is Tracey there?"

"Speaking; who is this?"

"I think you called me. My name is Milan."

"Oh, hi, how are you?" she said as if we were acquaintances. Somehow, I knew a bomb was about to drop.

"I'm fine. I was told that you had something to tell me about my husband."

"That's just it, honey. He's not your husband."

"Excuse me!"

"He can't be married to you when he's still married to me."

"What? You must have the wrong Justin because my Justin has never been married before."

"Well, honey, he lied. Look, I have no animosity toward you because you didn't know. Justin and me have been married for thirteen years and we have two children."

"You have to be mistaken now because Justin doesn't have any other children besides mine."

"I know about your son. And I also know that he's never around. How could you really believe that he was true? He doesn't even live with you! He told me everything about you but we were separated when he met you."

"This can't possibly be true!" I yelled in disbelief.

"Look, he doesn't even know that I called you; he wanted to tell you himself. I told him that I would give him some time because you have a baby together, but this has been going on long enough."

"So what am I supposed to do now?"

"Honey, I don't know, but he's my husband and we are back together now. If you need to speak with me anymore you can call me. But right now you really need to talk to Justin if you don't believe me."

"Maybe I will, okay?"

"Okay."

I hung up. What was happening to me? I didn't think that I was that bad of a person. I took care of my children and I believed that I was a good wife. I now understood why he started to act the way that he did. He was just trying to find a reason to leave me. How could he get me pregnant, have me believing that I was married, and the whole time he was married to someone else? I loved my son but now I hated his father. I should have known and that's the reason that I was so upset. I was so stupid and Devon was right. I couldn't even have him now as a friend because I was too confident that Justin and I were fine.

I just sat on the couch and cried, which was something that I seemed to do a lot of. I was tired of crying over men. I was through. I'd rather be alone than to keep being hurt that way.

At about five Devon and Samani walked in and I was still on the couch crying. Devon acted as if he didn't see me. He kissed Samani good-bye and left. That hurt me so much because maybe he really was getting over me and appeared to have lost all feeling for me. I knew I'd screwed up after the stunt pulled at the hospital. Samani came to the couch and put her hand on my shoulder.

"Mom, what's wrong?"

"Justin is married!"

"I know that, he's married to you."

"No, to someone else, before me."

"So, you're not really married?"

"No," I cried.

"Mom, it will be okay. He's been gone most of the relationship anyway. You don't need him. You'll be fine, okay?"

"I guess I will," I said, hugging her. She went upstairs to her room. I just stayed on the couch and stared at the wall. Again, I'd made the foolish choice of believing in him. I truly felt like the biggest asshole on the planet.

I waited for Justin but he never came and he never called. I figured that he wouldn't when he found out that

I'd spoken with his wife. I took off his ring and threw it out of the window. Twice I grabbed the phone and contemplated calling him but both times I talked myself out of it. I was tired of lying down and taking his shit. Enough was enough.

I went to bed that night feeling a little bit better, knowing that I could move on. I wasn't ever going to be Justin's fool again, or anyone else's for that matter.

Chapter Twenty-nine

Milan

Made Me Whole

I woke up the next morning with a headache. I got up slowly hoping it would lighten it up a little. The baby was awake, playing in his crib, and hadn't made a sound. After I found what I was going to wear I got the baby dressed and then I got dressed; then I went to open the store. The day was a normal day; customers came and went. Danell had some business to take care of so she was off for the day. All I could think about was my life and everything that I had been through since I came home. Maybe if I had stayed in Georgia I wouldn't have had to suffer.

In the passing weeks I tried very hard to get on with my life, but I missed having a man. Not for the sex but just for the love. I missed having Devon around, even as a friend, but he wouldn't talk to me now. Samani's pregnancy was going good and it was almost graduation time for her. Jayla was down for the summer and we were having fun together like we used to. When graduation day came Devon was there but of course he brought April along. I decided that I wouldn't ruin the day, so I left it alone. It hurt me though, not because he was with her but because he wasn't with me.

The way he was holding her, that should have been me. He was the man I needed to be with but it took someone else to hurt me for me to realize it. All I did was stare at him but every time he looked my way he quickly turned his head as if he was disgusted. After the graduation I gave a dinner at the house. Surprisingly Devon showed up alone.

"So you decided to show, huh?"

"Only for my daughter," he responded coldly.

"Devon, I didn't do you that wrong. I don't deserve to be treated this way. You act like you hate me."

"Oh, so now that he's not here you want me. What did he do this time, huh?"

"He's married to someone else!"

"Oh, really. Well, I told you that he would hurt you again but you didn't listen."

"I know, Devon, but I need you in my life now."

"Please, Milan, don't bore me. You don't really want me; you just want a man. So why don't you go find one?"

"I'm just going to walk away right now because I don't want to ruin her day and I guess you'll never forgive me. I guess I'm not worth it," I said as I walked away.

He stayed for about an hour and then he left without saying a word to me. I wasn't ready to give up yet because I believed that deep down, he still wanted me. But I decided to play his game.

About a month later I was in the mall with the baby. I'd let my loneliness confine me to the house long enough, so I decided to shop. It just so happened that I ran into Justin, who I definitely didn't want to see.

"Hi, how are you?" he said with a slight smile.

"I'm fine, as if you care."

"Milan, can we sit down and talk?"

"It wasn't that important to you to talk to me when your wife called."

"Look, I can explain that."

"There's no need to explain. I am moving on and doing fine without you."

"I want to explain. Her and me were separated when I met you. I didn't know that we were going to end up getting back together."

"But you said that you were never married. All that bullshit about never finding the right one. You had two children, Justin."

"I know, and I'm sorry. I didn't think I was going to fall in love with you and I definitely didn't think you would get pregnant."

"Well, if you didn't want to be with me why did you try?"

"Because when I saw you I wanted you. I knew I was married but you gave me your number. I didn't ask for it."

"Don't try to blame it on me, Justin. You didn't have to call and you didn't have to have sex with me. And maybe you didn't want a child but you have one and he needs a father."

"I know that!"

"Well, why haven't you called? He could have been dead and you acted as if you didn't care."

"I know that, too. Milan, I want to change. I want to be a good father to my son. I'm just going through some changes in my life right now and I need some time."

"Well, you know what? I won't be here and I hope that when he gets older he's not either." I started to walk away.

"Milan! Milan, wait."

I just continued to walk. I was through with him and I wasn't going to waste any more time. After I finished doing my shopping, I was putting the baby in the car and my cell phone rang. It was Samani.

"Mom. I need you. I think I'm in labor."

"Baby, I'm all the way in King of Prussia. I'll be there as soon as I can, okay?"

"Okay, Mom. I'm scared. Hurry!"

"I will."

I thought I was just as scared as she was. It wasn't time for this baby to come yet. I got in the car and was on my way. I got there in about a half hour. I gave Danell the baby and then I rushed in the room.

"I'm here, baby."

"Mom, it's not time yet. Why is this happening?"

"I don't know, baby. It'll be okay. All right?" I tried my best to console her while covering up my own fears. I was worried as any mother would be but now wasn't the time to fall apart.

Through all of the screaming and crying she had her baby, a little girl: four pounds, three ounces. The baby was beautiful but she was so tiny. Since she was premature she'd need to be hospitalized for some time. I couldn't imagine how difficult it would be to leave a child behind. I was determined to be as supportive as I possibly could.

Unlike my own relationships, hers was amazing. Dave, the father, was as supportive as one could ask for. I wasn't jealous but I was a little envious that she'd been able to achieve the one thing that I hadn't. A relationship was the one thing in my life that I hadn't been successful with. It was almost as if I was destined to be alone and although I wanted to believe differently, I didn't have any other choice. I was constantly back at square one: both single and bitter.

I gave up on love but I really needed it. I wanted to be satisfied with my life but I wasn't because I was missing something. I was missing the part of me that made me whole. I didn't know how long I could deal with it. There just had to be something better out there for me.

Chapter Thirty

Milan

No More Mistakes

Samani came to me with the news that she was moving in with Dave and that they were planning to get married. She stayed with me for about two more months after bringing the baby home and then she moved in with him. Dave was a few years older than her and already had his own place and car, which was a plus. I didn't think I would have fought for her to stay if he didn't. I started to help plan their wedding because they wanted to do it soon. This took a lot off my mind but then it still made me think of Justin. I got so mad at one point that I decided to take him to court for child support and since we weren't actually married I didn't need to file for a divorce. I didn't need any more but I was not going to let him get away from what he did to me. The least that he could do was come and see his son.

A court date was set. I went but he didn't show. I wasn't surprised but that was on him because I won the support that I deserved and that was my satisfaction. I continued with the wedding plans and the wedding came fast. It wasn't that big because she didn't want it to be. But it was beautiful. Devon came alone and he looked fine in his tux. He did speak to me but that was about it. At the reception

I walked over to Devon to talk. I felt like it was time that we got back on civil terms again.

"So, where's your girlfriend?"

"She's home."

"So, how have you been?"

"I've been fine, and you?"

"Lonely, but good."

"Well, maybe that's what you needed."

"That's a harsh thing to say."

"Well, that's how I feel."

"Fine, Devon. I'll leave you alone since that's what you want. But you don't have to be so evil to me."

"Well, that's how you treated me."

"No, I didn't."

"Yes, you did. And why do we have to keep disguising this? You don't care about me so stop acting like it."

"I do, never mind," I said as I walked away.

I couldn't stand him treating me this way and the confidence that I once had was quickly dwindling. He was showing me that he didn't feel the way I thought he'd felt about me. It was like he was digging a hole in my heart.

In the months that passed I tried to forget him but I was getting lonelier by the day. All I had was the baby; I got bored with the store as well. I let Danell run it most of the time. I was tired of playing this game with Devon so I decided to write him a long letter to tell him exactly how I felt. Maybe this would bring him around. But if it didn't I would know that I really had to get on with my life. I sat at the table and wrote.

Dear Devon,
I can't stop thinking about you so I decided to
write. Every day I sit and think of you, hoping that

you're okay, waiting for you to come back to me. If I had one wish it would be that we were together, forever, and no one else mattered. Growing up, falling in love was something that I dreamed of but when I found you again my dream came true. I never really wanted to fall so deep for you, but I'm completely in love. I always wanted to be with you; that's why not having you in my life hurts so badly. I no longer have someone to kiss me good night or tell me "I love you" before I go to sleep. I miss you so much and words really can't express what I feel inside. I just wanted to write this letter to tell you that I'm still here and whenever you are ready to be with me I'm ready too. I love you so much and I can't wait until the day when we are together again and I can make you happy. The day when we can express our love by making love and spending time together. This is completely the way that I feel about you and I know that I need you. I hope that when this letter reaches you our situation changes because I know that the longer we are apart the slimmer my chances are and I don't want to see or hear about you falling in love with anyone else again. I realize that I can't do much without you in my life holding me, kissing me, and loving me. The love I have is staying and I'll be here killing time waiting on you.

Love Always,
Milan

Months passed before I heard anything from Devon so I was moving forward, knowing that I'd said and done everything that I could. The store occupied my time and kept me from sitting at home sulking in misery. I was getting back to the old me and it actually felt great. It was a Thursday and I was just about to close the store when a flower delivery guy came. At first I thought these may have been from Justin and was about to refuse them but I read the card to see who it might be. It didn't have a name; it just said to come to the park at seven. I didn't know what to do. I told Danell, who insisted that I shouldn't go. It could have been a stalker or a murderer trying to get me alone. So many things were going through my mind all at once. My heart was telling me to go because it could be Devon finally ready to be with me, but my mind was saying it would be foolish to go out to the park alone. I gave in and decided to go. I didn't want to miss out on the chance to get my man back.

I got there about ten of seven and I didn't see anyone in sight. All I saw was a table with candles and food. I went over to the table and as soon as I sat down Devon came from behind a tree. My heart dropped. I smiled from ear to ear but I didn't want to get too excited because I didn't know what it was that he brought me out here to say.

"What is this about, Devon?"

"Look, I got your letter."

"And I mailed it three months ago."

"I know but I was being stubborn. I wasn't sure if you really loved me and I wanted you to prove it. Once I got your letter I knew that you were true. I thought that you would have given up on me but you didn't and I'm glad. I didn't really love April; she was just there. I know that we've been through a lot and it's going to take a lot of work for us to trust each other but if you are willing to try I am ready to give it a shot."

"Are you serious?" I began to cry. I was finally getting what I wanted. I was finally getting the man back who I was supposed to be with. After all of the reckless choices that I'd made in my life, coming out here at first appeared to be another one but ended up being the best choice of my life. I knew that things happened when they were supposed to, and sometimes we question God and what He has planned. I knew then, patience was one of the best qualities to have, along with persistence. Without those I would have still been alone and Devon most likely would have been with April.

I was able to accept their child and actually was pretty good at the stepmom role. I realized that she was a part of him and I was going to have to accept her, just as he did Justin Jr. We were the family I always hoped we'd be. My past was the past and all of the trouble and drama that I went through to get here was all worth it. I'd found self-worth and I'd found love. No more blaming everyone else for my mistakes.

ORDER FORM
URBAN BOOKS, LLC
97 N18th Street
Wyandanch, NY 11798

Name (please print):_____

Address: _____

City/State: _____

Zip: _____

QTY	TITLES	PRICE
	16 On The Block	$14.95
	A Girl From Flint	$14.95
	A Pimp's Life	$14.95
	Baltimore Chronicles	$14.95
	Baltimore Chronicles 2	$14.95
	Betrayal	$14.95
	Bi-Curious	$14.95
	Bi-Curious 2: Life After Sadie	$14.95
	Bi-Curious 3: Trapped	$14.95
	Both Sides Of The Fence	$14.95
	Both Sides Of The Fence 2	$14.95
	California Connection	$14.95

Shipping and handling: add $3.50 for 1st book, then $1.75 for each additional book.

Please send a check payable to:

Urban Books, LLC

Please allow 4-6 weeks for delivery

ORDER FORM
URBAN BOOKS, LLC
97 N18th Street
Wyandanch, NY 11798

Name (please print):_____

Address: _____

City/State: _____

Zip: _____

QTY	TITLES	PRICE
	California Connection 2	$14.95
	Cheesecake And Teardrops	$14.95
	Congratulations	$14.95
	Crazy In Love	$14.95
	Cyber Case	$14.95
	Denim Diaries	$14.95
	Diary Of A Mad First Lady	$14.95
	Diary Of A Stalker	$14.95
	Diary Of A Street Diva	$14.95
	Diary Of A Young Girl	$14.95
	Dirty Money	$14.95
	Dirty To The Grave	$14.95

Shipping and handling: add $3.50 for 1st book, then $1.75 for each additional book.

Please send a check payable to:

Urban Books, LLC

Please allow 4-6 weeks for delivery

ORDER FORM
URBAN BOOKS, LLC
97 N18th Street
Wyandanch, NY 11798

Name (please print):_____

Address: _____

City/State: _____

Zip: _____

QTY	TITLES	PRICE
	Gunz And Roses	$14.95
	Happily Ever Now	$14.95
	Hell Has No Fury	$14.95
	Hush	$14.95
	If It Isn't love	$14.95
	Kiss Kiss Bang Bang	$14.95
	Last Breath	$14.95
	Little Black Girl Lost	$14.95
	Little Black Girl Lost 2	$14.95
	Little Black Girl Lost 3	$14.95
	Little Black Girl Lost 4	$14.95
	Little Black Girl Lost 5	$14.95

Shipping and handling: add $3.50 for 1st book, then $1.75 for each additional book.
Please send a check payable to:
Urban Books, LLC
Please allow 4-6 weeks for delivery